"You call me a cheat and then you kiss me? Am I supposed to be flattered?" Melanie demanded.

"Do you think I like this...this attraction that's between us? I know you feel it as much as I do. Let's not play games. You want me as much as I want you," Monroe said.

"You can't call me dishonest, think negative things about me and expect me to welcome your advances. I don't play that game."

"Do you think I like the way you've intrigued me from the moment I met you?"

Monroe massaged the tense muscles in his neck and for a moment he studied her intently. He was mesmerized by the fiery, angry look in her eyes. He wanted to see her brown eyes blaze with a completely opposite emotion. He wanted...

"You're driving me crazy, you know that?"

Before she could respond, he opened the door and disappeared into the night.

CANDICE POARCH,

a nationally bestselling author, fell in love with writing stories centered around romance and families many years ago. She feels the quest for love is universal. She portrays a sense of community and mutual support in her novels.

Candice grew up in Stony Creek, Virginia, south of Richmond, but now resides in northern Virginia. Married twenty-nine years, she is a mother of three children. A former computer systems manager, she has made writing her full-time career, and she loves to hear from readers. Please visit her Web site at www.candicepoarch.net or write to her at P.O. Box 291, Springfield, VA 22150.

Candice Poarch
Sweet Southern Comfort

KIMANI
PRESS

Acknowledgments

Thank you Ben Rogers for information on alpacas, Sandy my career-long critique partner, my husband and my family for their continued support.

ISBN-13: 978-1-58314-788-7
ISBN-10: 1-58314-788-8

SWEET SOUTHERN COMFORT

www.kimanipress.com

Printed in U.S.A.

Dear Reader,

Sweet Southern Comfort is a story of mending fences, second opportunities and family feuds. Caught in the drama of a feud, children grow up afraid to form friendships, and adults are forced to live in the past. Even though living in a community with underlying tension can warp relationships, special friendships still cross the barrier. It takes Melanie and Monroe, both outsiders, to see the feud from both perspectives, but it takes much more for two hardheaded families to make peace.

Sweet Southern Comfort grew from my desire to write a story around two feuding families. Take a trip with me as we watch a community abandon the past to embrace the present.

Candice Poarch

Chapter 1

Melanie Lambert's gorgeous backside was pointed in the air as she shoved books onto a shelf. Through a glass-plated door, Monroe Bedford got a clear view of black slacks molded to her butt. Her short aqua top revealed a sliver of smooth brown skin at her lower back.

His hand gripped the door handle and he bit down the rage burning a hole in his gut.

He'd rather climb the Himalayas than go in Melanie's bookstore, and he hated heights. But his stubborn grandmother had insisted he remind

Melanie to bring some books to the rehabilitation center where she was recovering from a stroke. Every time Monroe asked for the names of the books, she'd only say "Melanie knows." From the moment he'd discovered Melanie was cheating his clueless grandmother, the very thought of her name set his back teeth on edge.

Swinging the door open, he crossed the threshold into the depths of what others might call a cheerful and inviting shop.

Melanie was standing in the section labeled Romance. His throat squeezed. When had that lead to anything but trouble? Women used their guile to paint an illusion, successfully drawing men like moths to their burning flames.

Melanie rose upright and her thick sable hair fell into place. With a welcoming smile, she glanced his way, her brown eyes meeting his. Before he could catch himself, her warmth tugged at him. Dull anger burned brighter in his brain and unwelcome fires of lust glowed in his veins. No wonder his grandmother was so easily conned.

"Welcome back," Melanie said.

Monroe nodded. "My grandmother said you're holding books for her. She asked me to get them."

"They're behind the counter. How is she?"

Melanie asked, taking quick strides to the cash register.

"Improving," Monroe responded without elaborating.

"I was going to take the books to her this evening when I visited."

"Her doctor is limiting visitors so she'll have more time for therapy. How much?" he said tightly, wanting to get the heck out of there and away from her mesmerizing smile as quickly as he could.

Frowning, she placed the books in a colorful bag and added coordinating tissue paper. "They're gifts."

"I'll pay for them." He took a soft calfskin wallet out of his back pocket.

"No, no. They're gifts from my daughter and me."

"I insist." His gaze touched hers and held. The Bedfords weren't going to owe her one copper penny. "How much?" he asked again. He glared at her. The way she and the shopkeepers were cheating his grandmother bordered on the criminal.

With a questioning look, Melanie added up the cost of the books and gave him a total.

"Monroe, is anything wrong?" Melanie asked, clearly baffled. But Monroe wasn't ready to reveal his findings. Not yet. "Is Mrs. Eudora okay?"

"She's fine." He quickly paid and left, well aware that her puzzled gaze followed him.

Melanie had talked his grandmother into building a small six-unit shopping plaza. Monroe's architect sister had even designed the units. He'd thought it would be the perfect thing to give his grandmother something to occupy her time without overtaxing her. The woman was always into something, when at her age she should be resting.

He should have kept closer tabs on his grandmother's affairs, but with his own nightmarish year, he'd let many things slide. A few days ago she'd asked him to deposit the tenants' checks into her bank account, and when he'd seen the piddling amount they paid for monthly rent, he was outraged.

Monroe opened the door to his car and slid onto the soft leather seat. On Monday he'd set up a meeting with her lawyer. One thing was for sure. This thievery wasn't going to continue. If it was the last thing he did, he was going to convince her to sell every single retail unit before he left town.

Gazing down Main Street, Monroe twisted the key in the ignition. As soon as the car roared to life, he put it in gear and pointed it out of Summer Lake, South Carolina, and toward the rehabilitation center, a half hour drive away.

* * *

An hour later, Melanie was still mystified over Monroe's strange and unfriendly behavior when her cousin, Gail Carson, burst into the store. She had the same caramel complexion as Melanie, but stood an inch shorter.

"Did you hear what happened?" she asked, out of breath.

"No…"

"The mayor has been telling everyone Monroe's going to sell the shopping center."

"Village Square?"

"What other shopping center is there in Summer Lake?"

Melanie's heart leaped. "Mrs. Eudora owns it and she'd never sell."

"Mrs. Eudora can't do anything from the sick bed, now can she? Monroe's taken over. The mayor's bragging about bringing in some interested buyers who plan to expand."

"This makes no sense. Why would Monroe sell? Are you sure it's not just a rumor? The mayor has been against this place from the get-go."

Gail sliced through the air with a dismissive hand. "People with money can do anything they want. They don't need a logical reason. Mama's so worried, she's having heart palpations." Gail's green skirt swirled around her legs as she paced back and forth. "I spent every dime I had for this place. Even mortgaged my house."

Melanie balled her hands into fists to keep them from shaking. She'd sunk her last penny into Melanie's Books & Treasures, too, but in a crisis somebody had to be the voice of reason. She could understand his selling if Mrs. Eudora wasn't going to improve, but she was expected to make almost a full recovery. Besides, Melanie handled all the small shopping center's problems.

"Don't start predicting doom and gloom. I'm sure it's not as bad as you think it is."

They heard raised voices outside and started for the door. Melanie's uncle, Milton Carson, and Elmore Hicks were arguing in front of the store for all the world to see. Elmore owned the store next door. The men still carried on a feud that should have died out decades ago. Melanie rushed outside.

"What's wrong with you? You're going to frighten the customers away."

"It's all his fault," her uncle Milton said, pointing a finger at Elmore. Elmore shot a disgusted glare at Milton. Neither man paid any attention to Melanie.

"Come inside my shop," Melanie demanded. "I don't have any customers right now."

Both men glared at each other before they strode angrily into her store.

"Why are you fighting?" Melanie asked.

"It's his fault," Uncle Milton bellowed. "His dizzy niece couldn't keep her skirt down and now we all have to pay."

"Leave Monroe's ex-wife out of this, Dad," Gail said.

"You don't know why he wants to sell," Elmore said, enraged. "You got no right talking about my family like that."

"None of us knows what's going on right now," Melanie reminded them. "So don't start with the accusations. We have more important issues."

"Like finding out exactly why he wants to sell and who wants to buy," Gail said. "We have ten-year leases, so even if he sold, we have our spaces for that long."

"Not exactly," Melanie warned. "If Village Square is sold, the leases are terminated in ninety days unless the buyer chooses to continue them."

"How could you agree to a lease like that, Melanie? We trusted you to work out a good deal with Mrs. Eudora." Elmore growled. Half a foot shorter than Milton, he crossed his arms over his barrel chest. "I've put every penny I've got in this place."

Uncle Milton slammed his fist on the countertop. "Don't you go blaming Melanie! Every time something goes wrong you blame her. You all but got down on your hands and knees begging her to talk Mrs. Eudora into renting you shop space. Shoulda known better than rent to a Hicks in the first place. It was right there in black and white. Didn't you read your lease before you signed it?"

"Daddy, please don't bring the feud into it." Gail sent Melanie a *here we go again* glance, then picked up the fallen books. The feud of 1951 was like a religion with Elmore and Milton.

The Carsons believed Elmore's father killed his wife—a Carson—back in 1951. There wasn't enough evidence to arrest him and the families had been at each other's throats ever since.

"We had to agree to the conditions of the lease because we're all startup businesses. None of us have track records," Melanie interjected.

"You're just going to have to talk to Mrs. Eudora," Uncle Milton said. "That's all there is to it."

"She isn't well enough to handle business." Nobody seemed to notice that Melanie was as worried as they were. She had a child to support. "Monroe told me the doctor restricted her visitors so I can't get anywhere near her." Melanie had never been so frustrated. Mrs. Eudora was improving, so she didn't understand why Monroe wouldn't let her visit the woman. She'd put so much energy and time into getting the shopping center built. Not to mention the fortune she'd spent on inventory for her store.

Melanie had hoped to run her store for the rest of her working career. To have it snatched away... She just couldn't fathom it.

"He knows she wouldn't sell to outsiders," Uncle Milton said, forcing Melanie out of her reverie.

"You've got to convince him not to sell, Melanie," Gail said.

"The mayor is already bragging about these new people bringing in name-brand stores. Somebody said they're going to make it three times bigger and they're not going to renew our leases. This will bankrupt me," Uncle Milton said. "You've got to do something."

"All right. All right. I'll talk to Monroe as soon as I can."

"It's just plain mean and disrespectful not letting anybody visit her," Gail said. "Where are his manners? With her family scattered all over the globe, who does he think looks after her?"

"Melanie, that's who," Uncle Milton said heatedly. "And this is a fine way to thank her." Her uncle patted Melanie's arm. "Don't you worry yourself, gal. We're just letting off steam." Everyone except Gail shuffled out the door with him.

For a second Melanie stared at the departing figures. A Carson and a Hicks hadn't been in the same room without raising fists in fifty-five years. The Carsons had even joined another church, refusing to worship with the Hicks. Could it be that they could unite for a single cause?

Not likely, Melanie thought. They'd forget about their camaraderie by tomorrow.

"What are you going to do about the anniversary party?" Gail asked.

"I told Mrs. Eudora we were going to delay it until she's better, to give her an incentive to get well quicker."

Gail nodded. "You're so good to that old woman. I better go help Mama. Call me after you talk to Monroe."

Melanie focused on the whimsical wind chimes Frank Jackson had made out of glass so delicate the birds, squirrels and frogs appeared to be floating. She needed to order some more. They sold out as quickly as she could stock them.

She sighed, glancing at the shelves of books and displays. Every time she thought things were going all right, life threw her a curve.

Melanie turned out the lights and closed up the shop. For a moment she peered inside, studying it the way she hoped a customer would. Huge plates of glass with white and royal-blue borders set off the storefront, with the name Melanie's Books & Treasures stenciled on the window inviting them inside.

Finally turning, she strolled across the street to her Cadillac SRX, one of the few luxuries she'd kept after her divorce. She plotted how quickly she could get into a long hot shower, slip under the covers into her bed and, for a little while, forget about all her troubles.

Melanie turned the key in the ignition. The motor roared to life and settled into a purr. Unfortunately, that hot shower would have to wait. She'd promised her daughter, Courtney, she'd be home by six-thirty to prepare chicken and dumplings—her favorite. Lowering her window, she breathed in the fresh air.

As Melanie drove the winding country road, the sun started to set and the brilliant orange cast shadows on the surrounding countryside. But thinking about the trouble Monroe and the mayor were causing dulled the beauty.

What was more, she knew she hadn't imagined the sharp and intimate spark between herself and Monroe on the day they'd met.

She first saw him weeks ago when Mrs. Eudora first had the stroke. Back then he was as pleasant as the rest of his family. She remembered their parting at the hospital when he'd taken her elbow and steered her out of the waiting area and into a deserted hallway. A charge zipped up Melanie's arm and spread through her body.

He braced a hand on either side of her and her pulse vibrated through her veins. He was standing close enough for her to feel the heat flaming from his body. Her gaze met his—and locked. A strong sensual current passed between them and he stared at her as if he were memorizing every pore. Her heartbeat increased, color stained her cheeks and her insides quivered with excitement as a slow flame burned through her body.

"Thank you," he said.

"For what?"

"For taking excellent care of my grandmother, and for your thoughtfulness. The coffee, sand-wiches—"

"—and me?" Melanie laughed, trying to break the sensual haze that gripped her. "Mrs. Eudora means a lot to me."

"The sentiment is mutual."

"I have to leave," he said.

Disappointed, Melanie said, "So soon?"

"Grandma's out of danger. Actually she's much better. They're moving her to a rehabilitation hospital tomorrow. But you know all that."

Melanie nodded.

"I have to finish up some business back home, but I'll be back in a few weeks."

Melanie nodded again. He gathered her hands in his, tugged her close. Melanie went willingly into his arms.

"Until I return…" He smoothed her hair back from her face, tilted her chin up with a long forefinger before his mouth came down to claim her. Melanie expected to feel his lips on hers, but he pressed a soft kiss on her cheek. His lips lingered only a second, and as she drew a shaky breath, he kissed her lips with a whispery soft touch. She was shocked by her own eager response.

Lord, Lord, Lord. She died and went to heaven when his arms closed around her completely, drawing her body into every part of his hard length.

He deepened the kiss and she held on to him as raw excitement surged through her system. But much too soon he let her go, and as he walked away, she felt as if part of her heart had been ripped from her.

He'd changed, and she didn't understand why. But she was going to find out. Tonight.

Monroe had never thought of his grandmother as frail. Her feisty nature duped people into thinking she was much younger than her eighty-two years. Dressed in a white gown and a pink bed jacket, she'd fallen asleep in a chair beside the bed. The pink brightened her face, but she looked so small…and frail…and every bit her age.

Until she opened her mouth. God, that woman loved to talk. Even the stroke hadn't stopped her. Perhaps it was the reason her speech had improved so quickly. Every time he visited, she asked about the "charming" Melanie. Monroe swore beneath his breath, and his grandmother suddenly jerked awake. Her eyes met his and he forced himself to smile.

"Have you been here long?" Her voice was slightly slurred as a result of the stroke, but it still held its commanding timbre.

"Just arrived." Approaching her, he leaned over her chair and kissed her soft cheek, then set the bag of books on her table. Pulling up a chair, he sat beside her and took her hand in his.

"Are these my books? I thought Melanie was bringing them. Have you talked to her?" she asked Monroe.

He bit off an oath. "She doesn't want you to worry about business right now. Everyone wants you to get your rest so you can recuperate quickly."

"They're trying to keep me here forever. The nurse brought up the flowers from the tenants. She said Melanie left them at the desk. I asked her why she didn't come up to my room."

"The doctor limited your visitors. We want you to get your strength back so you'll be good as new."

"Bunch of baloney. I want to see Melanie. Bring her with you on your next visit."

Like hell. Monroe sighed, struggling for patience. "Grandma…"

"She's a wonderful girl, Monroe. Nothing like Dorian. I told you Dorian wasn't right for you before you married her, didn't I? But did you listen?"

"Yeah, yeah. Don't elevate your blood pressure over it."

"I say good riddance. You're better off without the tramp."

"You're pushing it, Grandma. Leave it alone."

"I will not. What kind of woman takes up with your best friend? Melanie would never do that. She's got character. She's got grit."

"Like you know so much about her."

"I do."

Monroe gave up. Even half-sick, his grandmother was a force to be reckoned with. If she were well, he'd battle with her. For now, it was best to let her wind down on her own before she worked herself into another stroke.

But Eudora wouldn't drop it. "Have you talked to Melanie? Is everything all right at Village Square?" she asked.

"It's running fine."

"Good. You keep a check on things. Make sure they're okay. What else is going on in town?"

"Nothing's going on. Nothing ever does."

"That's what you think, boy. Never thought a grandson of mine would be so clueless."

"What's got you so moody? Stop worrying about the plaza." She was sick in the hospital and still worried about those damn stores. He *had* to convince her to sell.

"I'm not moody," she said. "I'm sure Melanie is keeping an eye on things."

He was sure she was.

"I'm a little tired. Think I'll get ready for bed."

Monroe stood to help her, but she pushed him away.

"I can do it myself." She gripped the walker with both hands and used her stronger leg to pull herself to a standing position. Then, balancing herself, she took quick little steps to the bathroom.

Monroe stayed until she was safely in bed.

"Get a good night's sleep," he said, tucking the covers around her shoulders. "I'll be back in the morning, Grandma."

"Don't run yourself ragged over me," she said, snuggling comfortably into her pillow. "You need more in your life than work and an old woman. One day you're going back to wherever. Be nice if you had a good woman on your arm." She yawned. "Then again, you might stay."

"Women, the answer to all of man's problems," he said in a voice laced with sarcasm.

As he walked out of the hospital, the mayor intercepted him. Monroe stifled an oath.

"Good to see you, Monroe." He slapped Monroe on the shoulder and pumped his hand as if he were canvassing votes for an election. All he lacked was a big cigar.

"How's Mrs. Bedford?"

"Improving."

"Good, good." He rocked back on his heels. "I'm really worried about her."

"I appreciate your concern."

"I'd like a word with you if you have the time."

Monroe glanced at his watch. "I have a few minutes. Let's talk on our way to the parking lot." He started walking and the mayor fell in step with him.

"I think it's a good decision to sell Village Square. Bartholomew, Inc. can do wonderful things for this town. The oldest son will be here next week. He wants to see the shops and, since it's spring break, he'll see how busy this place can get."

"I haven't agreed to sell. Especially not before I discuss it with my grandmother." The mayor didn't need to know his business.

His expression grave, the mayor said, "Your grandmother hasn't been herself the last couple of years. She's started to cling to Melanie Lambert. That woman has an unnatural control over Mrs. Bedford. I hate to say this, but I believe your grandmother's getting senile."

Senile my foot. "You wouldn't say that if you heard the way she lit into me."

"Old folks are just grouchy. But it doesn't keep people from taking advantage of them when family isn't around to keep an eye on things. It's a crying shame. I tried my best to counsel her, but she won't listen to me. Melanie's control is too solid."

He had a point there, Monroe thought. "Why didn't you call my father or me?"

"Didn't know how to contact you. And Mrs. Bedford would have had my hide."

Monroe tightened his lips in anger. In the last two years, he'd been so busy with his divorce and the hostile buyout of his company, he hadn't seen his grandmother as often as he should have. He didn't necessarily like the mayor, but he could see by his grandmother's financial records that she'd been taken advantage of.

"I think it's a good thing you aren't allowing visitors," the mayor continued. "The tenants would only upset your grandmother."

Monroe reached his car. "Thank you for stopping by."

"Is there anything you'd like me to tell Bartholomew?"

"No."

"Let me know if I can help you and your grandmother in any way. She was a good woman."

"She's still alive," Monroe said.

"Of course. Of course."

It was only after Monroe got in the car and slammed the door that the mayor started to walk away. That man was getting to be a pain in the backside about the shopping center. Although Monroe had power of attorney, he wasn't about to make a decision like selling the plaza until his grandmother was well enough to discuss it with him. It still belonged to her. And he knew how it felt when people sold something you loved against your wishes.

Eighteen months ago he'd had a wife and a company. Now he had neither.

They were four friends—Monroe, Peter, Eric and Aaron—who'd met their freshman year at Morehouse. And their friendships had remained strong after they'd graduated, so much so that they'd decided to go into business together. They'd forged their talents and expertise to start an engineering company. Business had exploded and grown at an astonishing rate, much faster than they'd ever dreamed possible.

When Monroe had visited his grandmother one summer, he'd seen his old high-school sweetheart, Dorian Hicks. They'd hit it off as if they'd never parted. Within six months, they were married.

Eighteen months ago, he discovered that while he

was burning the midnight oil working, Aaron and Dorian were having an affair. Monroe immediately filed for a divorce. It came through a year ago.

He knew his partner Aaron was a ladies' man. But he never expected him to betray their friendship or put their business in jeopardy.

Monroe had ruthlessly put it behind him. He didn't miss Dorian. It was more the idea of that perfect little nuclear family that seemed as unreachable as the stars above.

Offers for buyouts were constant. Each partner owned one fourth of the company. They thought it would protect them from a takeover. But they were more than owners. Eric was company CEO. Peter was vice president in charge of accounting. Smooth-talking Aaron was in charge of sales and marketing. Monroe, with his engineering background, was in charge of their scientific division. It seemed the perfect combination. But not for long. When Dorian left Monroe for Aaron, Peter had pushed Monroe to sell the company and the others had backed him.

Monroe had wanted to keep the business intact. But he'd stood alone.

Monroe gazed into the gathering sunset, and couldn't help but think of his ex. Dorian grew up in Summer Lake. Her family lived there—grandparents, parents, sisters and brothers. All the others were still married. She'd represented stability. He used to picture himself with her surrounded by a huge family fifty years down the road. It might have seemed boring to some, but he grew up a military brat, roaming from base to base. He longed for something constant. He craved roots.

He had two brothers and two sisters. None of them were married, and they were scattered all around the globe. He was lucky if he saw any of them once in two years. The only constant in his life was his grandmother's house. It was the only place of familiarity, which was the reason he'd refurbished the old family home in the first place.

So now he headed to the place he'd designed as a retreat for his family. It was a place they all could gather and call home.

Chapter 2

Monroe owned a house less than half a mile from Eudora's. He'd figured someday a family member would have to move close by to look after her. With that in mind, when the lease for the colonial revival where his great grandparents had lived had come up for renewal, Monroe had bought and renovated it. Only he hadn't figured he would be the person moving back to Summer Lake.

Huge live oaks lining the long driveway were a picture worth taking. The massive displays of azaleas and the beautiful rose garden were giving them competition. The tall symmetrical columns welcomed him. One of the things he loved most about the house was the double-paned windows. When he looked through them, the view seemed like a framed painted landscape.

Monroe climbed out of his car and noticed bright lights from another car coming up the drive. It stopped behind his and when the door slowly opened, Pearl Seaborn struggled to get out. He went over to assist her.

"Glad you're here," she said. "I have a bag for Mrs. Eudora. I washed her clothes for her."

"She'll be glad to get them."

"In the back seat," Pearl said.

Monroe opened the back door and hauled out his grandmother's designer suitcase. Mrs. Pearl supervised the women who cleaned both his grandmother's and his house weekly. She had a kindly face, but she also enjoyed her own delicious cooking too much. And the woman loved to talk, so Monroe always made an effort to be someplace else on cleaning day.

"Thanks for laundering her things," he said as another car came up the driveway. Maybe she would get the hint and leave.

"Anytime," she mumbled, but she followed him

to the front porch and turned to look on eagerly as the driver parked in the yard.

Melanie climbed out. Desire and need hit Monroe immediately. He drew in an angry breath. She still had power over him.

In the evening, when the average woman looked whipped by the day's events, Melanie looked fresh and pretty in her teal top and black slacks.

"Well, aren't you a sight for sore eyes," Pearl said, obviously happy to capture an unsuspecting ear. "What brings you out here?"

"Good to see you, Mrs. Pearl."

Resigned to the women's intrusion, Monroe led everyone inside to the family room.

"You still got some of that iced tea I made for you?" Pearl asked Monroe as she made herself comfortable on the family room couch.

"Sure." While Monroe went to get it, the women struck up a conversation.

"You poor child," Pearl said to Melanie. "If you aren't stuck right in the middle of the biggest mess."

"Everything's fine, really," Melanie assured her.

"The feud is becoming bigger than the tornado that tore through five years ago, with no end in sight."

Monroe set a glass of tea in front of each of the women.

"You know all about the feud, don't you, Monroe?"

"Something about a Hicks killing a Carson decades ago." He sat in a chair across from the ladies.

"That doesn't even begin the tale," she said, settling in for juicy gossip. "'Round 1951 Mark Hicks married Rebecca Carson. Now, she was dead before either of you were born. You probably saw pictures of her, Melanie."

"Uncle Milton has plenty of them."

"Well, Mark died just a few years ago. You may not remember him since you were little when you left, Melanie. But Monroe, you probably saw him when you spent summers with your grandmother when you were a little thing."

"I do," Monroe said, twisting irritably in his seat, but Pearl didn't notice.

"I can recall it like it was yesterday. Rebecca was a sweet child, but young and flighty. Her daddy didn't want her to marry Mark, but he loved her and gave her anything she wanted."

Monroe glanced at Melanie. She must have heard the story a thousand times. Pearl repeated it to anyone who'd sit still long enough to hear it.

"Ain't right to spoil a girl that way," she continued. "Course Mark got himself a job, telling anybody who'd listen that he wasn't like his folks. He was going to better himself. Yeah, he sure did that." She took a fortifying sip of tea.

"I don't want to keep you, Pearl, if you…" Monroe started.

She waved a hand. "Got plenty of time. Rebecca's folks had money, you see. The Carsons were always a hardworking family, back then and now. Not a lazy one in the bunch. And that no account Mark knew it." Pearl looked into the fireplace as if she were seeing it anew. "Lord they put on a grand affair. Prettiest and biggest wedding this town ever seen, to this day. You seen pictures of the wedding, Melanie.

"I tell you, Rebecca was a pretty thing. And that sorry Mark Hicks didn't have a pot to piss in. Quit his job soon after the 'I do.' But the Carsons were land rich. Rebecca's daddy gave her two hundred acres so Mark could take care of her, for all the good it did."

Melanie nodded.

"You can't be nice to some folks. That Mark was as mean as a snake. An evil man if there ever was one. He mistreated that poor child. Before the ink dried on the wedding license, I tell you, he was jumping in the sack with that tramp, Lucinda Beavers. Your uncle tell you about that?" she asked Melanie.

Melanie nodded, again. Knowing Milton, Monroe imagined he repeated it over and over.

"I used to see bruises Rebecca tried to cover up when she came to church. She suffered with that man and he finally killed her two years after the wedding," she said quietly and more than a little indignantly. "He said she fell off the roof to her death, but we know he pushed her. He wanted her out of his life. And he found a way to make it happen. Had her climbing that ladder to hand him some tools up on the roof of that shack he moved her into, he said. You should have seen those big crocodile tears pouring down his face, but everybody knew better." She shook her finger for emphasis. "He killed her as sure as I'm sitting here today."

"Why wasn't he arrested?" Monroe asked.

"He was lazy but he wasn't no fool. He made sure nobody was around. Couldn't prove he killed her."

"So they aren't really sure."

Clearly indignant she said, "Of course we're sure. We all know he did it. Old man Carson wanted his land back, too, and rightfully so. But wasn't a thing he could do. Rebecca's brothers beat the stuffing out of Mark, and they been fighting ever since." She shook her head. "The Carsons and the Hicks. Mark up and married Lucinda less than a year later. Didn't give poor Rebecca time to turn cold in her grave, bless her soul. And he never did no better than to scratch out a living on that land. Was always poor as Joe Turkey. But let me tell you something. A no account is a no account, you hear me." Pearl's voice rose and she leaned forward in her chair for emphasis.

"Mark never amounted to nothing. He was lazy as a house cat and he died that way. And the chip don't fall too far from the block. Them three children he and Lucinda whelped wasn't no better, except for Elmore."

Ready for the story to end, Monroe cleared his throat, but it didn't stem Pearl's diatribe. In the city, he would have had her on her way. But things worked differently in the country; you were expected to show respect to your elders.

"That boy worked from the time he was a little thing. He was collecting eggs from the chickens and slopping the hogs when he was no more than five or six. And he was the youngest. When he growed up and made a little money, he bought his brothers out. His parents had passed on by then. Now he owns the whole two hundred acres and more. He's a good soul. And he's doing well with that pig farm selling them hams. Lord those hams are something to smack your lips around. But family is family. He's still a Hicks and nobody's ever gonna forget it." Her gaze swung to Monroe. "I'm just sorry you got mixed up in the mess by marrying a Hicks, Monroe. Coulda told you it wasn't going to work. And I don't care what they say. It's her fault she left. There isn't a thing wrong with you."

Face flushed, Monroe hopped out of the seat and grabbed Mrs. Pearl's elbow, barely able to contain his anger. He felt Melanie staring at him, and she looked embarrassed. Which made his predicament even worse. His divorce from Dorian was none of Mrs. Pearl's damn business. The heck with manners.

He plucked Mrs. Pearl's purse from the floor and thrust it at her. "Getting late," he said, halfway lifting her from her seat. "Melanie and I have business to discuss. Let's talk another time."

Mrs. Pearl was still talking.

"All right. I'm going," she said as he guided her toward the door. "Dorian could turn a man's head. But she was no good just like her kin."

"It's all in the past," Monroe said.

"I'm confident things will change one day," Melanie responded hastily. "The feud won't last forever."

"That'll be a cold day in hell." Pearl shook her head, her gray hair reflecting in the light as she tried to turn toward Melanie, but Monroe kept her moving. "Elmore ain't never giving up that land. And the Carsons ain't gonna rest till they get it back. So they're just like them folks over in the Middle East. Now you tell me how there's ever gonna be an end to that feud. You're dreaming, girl. And since you're a Carson and planning on running that store right here, you're gonna be forever stuck right where you are. Dead center. Don't matter that you left here when you were ten and the feud don't mean nothing to you. You're still a Carson."

"Goodbye, Mrs. Pearl," Melanie called out.

In the corner, the grandfather clock striking the hour sounded like an explosion.

"Lord have mercy. Didn't know it was so late. Got a million things to do for the Blessing on the Lake on Saturday," she said. "You all coming, aren't you?"

"I'll be there," Monroe said.

"I know you're coming, Melanie. Monroe, see that your grandma gets those clothes right away."

Grateful she was finally out of the house, Monroe said, "I'll take them to her tomorrow."

"Just drop off the ones needing laundering at

my place and I'll take care of 'em for you. Don't take them to the cleaners now. Your grandma likes the sweet smell of the lake breeze in her sheets. You can't get that in a dryer, so I hung her nightgowns on the line. Help her sleep nights."

"I appreciate it." Although he didn't know the difference. He'd been brought up on dryers and they worked fine for him.

Pearl drove off and he had to go back into that room and hope that Melanie had enough tact to ignore Pearl's reference to his wife. The fact that he was attracted to Melanie made the situation even worse.

"How is Mrs. Bedford?" she asked when he returned.

"She's well."

"Give her my regards, please."

"I will." He settled in the Queen Anne chair again. He shifted in his seat so that he was facing her. His gray eyes were flat and cold, and they chilled Melanie to the bone.

His demeanor wasn't encouraging for discussing business, especially if she wanted a positive response. Unfortunately, Melanie had no choice but to plunge ahead anyway.

"I'm here on behalf of the tenants' association,"

she started. "We're concerned about the group interested in buying Village Square. The tenants have invested a lot in their shops and they're worried that you'll sell and they'll lose their space."

"You mean they're worried they won't be able to take advantage of these people the way they have my grandmother."

"Excuse me?" She struggled to hide her confusion.

"Yes, Ms. Lambert. I've been through my grandmother's financial records. It didn't take long to realize she's getting a mere fraction of the value of those units."

"I'm aware of that, but—"

"Now that I'm taking care of her estate, that's going to stop. You should be arrested."

"What are you talking about?" *How dare he!* Confusion quickly turned to anger.

"None of the family was here to look after my grandmother before, but I'm here now. Fleecing senior citizens is old school. I don't know how you can live with yourself."

"I'm not taking—"

"You may be the princess of Village Square, but you won't be able to wrap her around your finger any longer."

"I haven—"

"She's spent a fortune on that complex. And for her to receive a piddling amount in return is appalling. I'm going to go through her records with a fine-tooth comb. And if I find any indication that you've cheated her more than you already have, I'll have you arrested."

Seething with rage, Melanie couldn't sit another moment. She stood and leaned toward him. This person was the evil clone of the man who'd been here weeks ago. It couldn't possibly be the same man.

"Mr. Bedford, no one has taken advantage of your grandmother. She agreed to let us pay a reduced rent for two years. This is a small town. It took everything the tenants had to stock the stores. And we opened during the slow season. Your grandmother is giving us time to recoup some of our start up costs before she starts charging full rent." She took deep breaths to force herself to calm down. It worked only a little. "I know the mayor has been talking to you. He's been against this development from the start. None of the people in the tenants' association voted for him. He dislikes all of us."

"And with good reason." Monroe was on his feet, too, and they glared at each other across the coffee table.

"Don't worry, we've set up the terms of the lease so that she'll receive every penny she's owed."

"There's no doubt of that. I'll see that she's paid."

Melanie poked him in the chest. "You're making a lot of accusations, mister. Have you discussed this with your grandmother?" Melanie asked. She wanted to rip that smug look off his face.

"In her state, I'm not going to worry her with business and neither are you."

His voice was absolutely emotionless, and it chilled her.

"If you had discussed this even in a casual conversation, her story would be completely different from the mayor's." Melanie sighed deeply. "Look, I'm asking you to wait until Mrs. Eudora is better before you decide. You'll bankrupt not just me, but the other tenants, as well. If another company takes over and doesn't renew our leases, or if they charge more than we can afford, it will be a disaster. The locals need every advantage they can get."

"No promises. You'll have my decision after my accountant looks over my grandmother's records."

Melanie nodded. "Contrary to whatever the mayor has told you, we haven't taken advantage of Mrs. Eudora. She's a wonderful woman who's done a lot for this town, and for me. We're grateful.

I'm asking you to keep an open mind. The mayor has his own agenda—and it isn't for the town's benefit. Or your grandmother's."

"Save your speech for someone who'll believe you."

"Or maybe someone with a heart," Melanie rejoined, regretting the words as they left her mouth. Sometimes she spoke before she thought, but fury almost choked her as his harsh words echoed in her brain. Nobody, but nobody, accused her of thievery, or of taking advantage of the elderly. "Let's get one thing straight. I'm not a thief. You should have had your accountant look things over *before* you started slinging allegations."

"Consider this meeting over." Monroe motioned for her to precede him to the door.

Both fear and anger knotted inside her. She opened her mouth, then closed it before she said something else she'd regret later.

Fire flashed in her eyes as she turned and marched ahead of Monroe. Fire that reached all the way to his center.

Gravel scattered as she tore out of the yard. Monroe stood in the doorway watching her tail-lights disappear. He still felt the impression of her finger in his chest. She might have the town fooled, but he knew better. He'd forced himself not to watch Melanie's rigid shoulders or attractive backside, or be enticed by the subtle scent of her perfume. He wouldn't be swayed by beauty. He knew better than most that beauty could be deceiving.

Monroe thought about Melanie that Friday afternoon as he hopped out of the truck and joined his farm manager with the rest of the crew in the alpaca pen.

After his retirement, Monroe's grandfather had skipped from organic gardening to creating an engine that would run five hundred miles on a gallon of gas. Neither venture had met with success. He'd finally settled on raising and showing exotic animals, namely alpacas from Peru. After his death, Monroe's grandmother had wanted to sell them, but Monroe had bought them from her. Why, he didn't have a clue. He'd hired Anthony Carson, a farm manager, to take care of them.

A couple of the workers hadn't shown up, and they were seriously shorthanded for the shearing of the alpacas, but the impending work couldn't keep Monroe's mind from switching to Melanie.

He hadn't planned to reveal that he knew about her trickery, but Mrs. Pearl's tortuous story had rattled him and, on top of that, Melanie had had the nerve to plead her case. He wasn't listening to another tale.

Melanie had seemed so genuine, he thought. The mayor was obviously as fake as the next politician, but Monroe still believed something was shady with the plaza business. But his grandmother hated the mayor and loved Melanie. And she asked about Melanie every day. She'd insisted he bring Melanie and her daughter to visit her. He didn't know how he was going to make it happen. After their argument, he was certain she'd rather crack open his skull than go anywhere with him.

Monroe began the sweaty work of shearing the alpacas. They hated the heat as much as he did.

While he helped hold the animal, the shearer sheared the line of belly hair, the legs, below the tail, from the tail to the belly and up towards the front and the spine. Before the shearer completed the animal, Monroe heard laughter. He waited until it was finished and Jewel began gathering the fleece before he glanced up. A pint-sized girl on the back of one of his horses, Rainshadow, was trotting down the path with her flying ponytail peaking from beneath her English hat. She wore jeans with her riding boots.

The girl and horse sprinted as if they belonged

together, as if they were a team. For a moment he stood mesmerized. What would it feel like to be part of a team of anything? Horse and rider approached him and the girl slowed Rainshadow to a walk until they stopped beside him.

"She's my little cousin who visits the farm from time to time. Mrs. Eudora doesn't mind that she rides the horses and plays with the alpacas," Anthony said. Jewel assisted the shearer on the next alpaca, and Monroe moved away from the pen to the fence.

"Hi," the girl called out. Rainshadow sidestepped and she bent over to rub the horse's side, gently cooing to the horse. "I'm exercising her. She's been cooped in the stable with no one to ride her."

"Mighty kind of you."

"I'm Courtney. Are you Mr. Bedford?"

"I am."

"I haven't been by lately and Rainshadow missed me," she said proudly. "I couldn't wait for Friday."

Monroe scowled. The skittish alpaca he was holding by the neck had broken away and run to the fence in the far corner.

"It's so fun here, but it's not the same without Mrs. Eudora here. I miss her. How is she?"

"Better," Monroe said, thinking the girl was

a breath of fresh air, but she needed to stop disturbing them.

"I have something for her but I haven't been able to take it to her yet."

"Bring it by and I'll see she gets it."

"Will you?"

"Sure."

"I'll get my mom to bring me by tomorrow. Can I help shear the alpacas?"

"No, you can't," Anthony said. "Please stop interrupting our work."

Monroe needed to find out which Carson she belonged to. Probably one of Milton's grandkids.

Anthony frowned at her. "Does your mama know you're here?"

"Not exactly."

Anthony narrowed his eyes. "What's going on?"

"She thinks I'm at my cousin's. I'm going over there later after I help with the alpacas and ride Rainshadow."

"And how are you going to get there?" Anthony asked.

"You're taking me?" she asked with a sheepish smile pretty enough to melt ice. "You're not shearing Tanya are you?" Tanya was an alpaca she'd named.

He shook his head. "You're going to show her at the 4-H fair so she can't be sheared."

"Let me shear Joy, please." Obviously Joy was another favored alpaca. Did the girl name all the animals?

"We're talking about your mama, young lady. I'll call her and let her know you're here."

The bright smile got even more brilliant as she climbed down from the horse and opened the fence to go inside. Tanya trotted over to her and she hugged the animal. "Thanks, Anthony. You're not going to sell Tanya are you?" she asked Monroe.

"Mrs. Eudora said not to," Anthony said, "but Monroe has the final word. Tanya belongs to him."

Courtney turned imploring eyes on him. "Please don't sell her. She's wonderful. Her coat is beautiful. Just look at it. It'll make beautiful sweaters one day."

"We'll see," Monroe said. It was mischievous heartbreakers like her that made him wish he and his wife had had at least one child during their short marriage.

Anthony flicked the child's ponytail. "Go ride Rainshadow some more. I'll help you with Joy later on."

Monroe threw a stern glance at Courtney. "I guess you expect to keep Joy's fleece?"

"Yeah." Her brilliant smile filled his heart with pleasure.

She mounted her horse but stayed to watch the shearing.

"What's this I hear about you charging to help classmates with their math?" Anthony asked.

"Our math teacher is the worst teacher I ever had. But I can follow the book so I help the other students."

"For a price."

She shrugged. "It's a job."

"Somebody told me you charge the Hickses double."

"I'm a Carson. Uncle Milton said I should have charged them more."

"That's my girl! But your mama wouldn't like it, so let it be our little secret."

Monroe scoffed. "What're you doing? Teaching them to feud from the cradle?" No wonder the feud was still going on.

Chapter 3

College kids on their spring break were driving down the coastline to the Florida, Carolina and Georgia beaches, and all day the bookstore had hummed with customers. Melanie had scheduled both of her part-time helpers and they'd worked with only short breaks. She didn't allow herself the luxury of a break. It was now nine-thirty and she hadn't had a bite to eat since breakfast. It was time to close up shop.

Melanie ran out the door at the same time as Gail.

"Hi, Melanie. I thought my shop was the last one to close."

"I don't think anyone closed early," Melanie said.

"Where's Courtney?"

"Girl, my heart had nearly dropped to my stomach when Anthony called earlier to tell me Courtney had shown up at the Bedford farm after school, riding down the lane with Rainshadow, no less. Evidently Monroe hadn't been there. He'd have tossed Courtney off his property."

"You still angry with Monroe?" she asked.

"Not even Scrooge would be mean to Courtney."

"I wouldn't put it past him. Someone should give him and the mayor a one-way ticket on a train heading North. He's no good for the town."

"Somebody should run against him," Melanie said.

"Why don't you? You'd make a great mayor."

"I don't have time. Besides, it's just the excuse my ex will need to accuse me of not spending enough time with Courtney, or that I'm an unfit mother."

"Like he has room to talk. We'll talk about it later. I'm running late."

"Hot date?"

"The first in many months."

"Have fun."

Lakeside Diner had been a fixture in Summer Lake for as long as Melanie could remember. She glanced at the rows of cars parked in the diner's lot, only a few short steps from the plaza. From the looks of it, she was going to have a long wait, but it was getting late and she didn't feel like cooking.

Opening the restaurant door, the tiny bell rang. The frazzled hostess didn't even look up. Some of the pictures of lake scenes that had graced the walls for decades had been replaced by newer prints. And although the seats and tables were old and scarred, the atmosphere was full of vitality.

"Sorry, it's a zoo. Table for one?" the hostess asked. When Melanie nodded, she said, "There's a half hour wait. Why don't you go to the bar and order a drink. You look like you need one as badly as I do. I'll come get you when your table's ready." Lakeside didn't hand out fancy pagers like the city restaurants.

Five minutes later, Melanie closed her eyes with the first cool swallow of a margarita easing down her parched throat. She lived for moments like this, she thought as she watched the youngsters horsing around at a table next to her. They waved and she waved back. She recognized the ones who'd stopped by her store earlier to buy books and a surprising number of figurines. She loved the energy. Energy meant business. More business meant profits.

She'd just taken her second sip when the hostess rushed over.

"Melanie, be a doll will you? We only have one table available right now. No telling when you'll get one, but Monroe Bedford said he'd share his with you. We're asking the locals to share because we have a mile-long line outside. Looks like a hundred cars just pulled in."

The last person Melanie wanted to share a table with was Monroe. But she didn't want to stand over a hot stove, either.

Drink in hand, she followed the hostess to the table with as much enthusiasm a trip to the dentist would bring. Scowling, Monroe stood when she sat.

"Do you ever smile?" she asked, still miffed at his accusations.

His scowl deepened, if that was possible.

"Guess not." She snapped the menu open. "Maybe I'll order a Coke. The fizz will help with indigestion."

"You could always wait another hour for a table."

"Don't tempt me."

"Look, we can try to get along for the space of one meal."

I don't think so. "How is Mrs. Eudora?"

Frustration flickered across his face. "Asking about you."

She bet that annoyed the heck of out him.

"I'll visit her tomorrow, then. With your permission, of course."

Ignoring her sarcasm, he said, "I'll take you. And your daughter. She wants to see both of you."

She stared at him, startled and surprised. *Sit in a car with him for forty-five minutes. I don't think so.* "What did Mrs. Eudora do to get you to change your mind? Threaten to disown you?"

He glowered at her, then focused on the menu. "*I'll* drive Courtney there, thank you."

His gaze jerked up. "Courtney?"

"Yes."

"The one who thinks she owns Rainshadow and half of my alpacas?"

Melanie chuckled uneasily. "That's the one."

"Figures."

The heavy dose of sarcasm piqued her anger and her eyes narrowed.

"What's that supposed to mean?"

"Ready to order?" the young waitress asked,

totally ignorant of the tension. Pencil hovering above her pad, she let out an impatient sigh when they didn't respond immediately.

"I'll take the pork-chop special," Melanie said, still glaring at Monroe.

"All gone," the woman said.

Melanie tore her gaze to the waitress. "How can you be out of the special already?"

"Look around you. All the hotels up and down 95 are already full and the college kids have crashed here. Figure half of 'em'll sleep in the parking lot tonight. Brian already asked me if I'll work till two in case they want sodas or a sandwich later on. That crazy man's leaving a serving window open all night. Like he can't stand missing out on a couple of dollars."

"I'll take the chicken," Melanie said. Maybe she'd open at six tomorrow morning just in case someone needed reading material for their trip. The young waitress might not understand the importance of raking every dime she could, but Melanie did.

The woman's gaze jerked to Monroe. "And you, sir?"

"The flounder."

When the waitress walked away, Melanie

returned to the conversation as if it had never paused. "What is it now? You don't want Courtney riding your horse or playing with the alpacas? You don't want her on your land?"

"I don't care. They seem to like her as much as she likes them. Besides, nobody else can ride Rainshadow," he said.

"That's understandable. Courtney helped nurse her back to health. Rainshadow was mistreated by her previous owner, but she gets nothing but love from my daughter."

"I know. If it's one thing I can't stand is someone mistreating defenseless animals. If you don't like them, stay away from them."

"Well bring out the band. Finally, we agree on something."

Monroe leaned back in his seat, carefully studying her. He didn't know whether he wanted to strangle her or kiss her. "That sharp tongue ever get you in trouble?"

"Not yet."

There was definitely something intriguing about a woman who spoke her mind and didn't expect a man to read it. He would always know where he stood with this sharp-tongued witch. If only, he thought. If only he could trust her.

He couldn't help the spark of interest that swept through him. The red top with the deep V she was wearing did amazing things to his imagination. It didn't help that she looked striking in red.

"Mrs. Eudora said you'd recently sold your engineering company."

The loss still stabbed his heart. He nodded.

"Did you enjoy your work?"

"Very much."

"In that case, why did you sell?" Melanie couldn't envision selling her shop willingly. She loved it too much.

"I was one of four partners. The other three wanted to sell. I didn't." He shrugged. "I was outvoted."

"I'm sorry." She reached across the table and patted his hand. "I know how it feels to lose something important, something you love. When you love your job, the work is more than getting through the dreaded eight hours to pay the mortgage or rent."

Monroe hadn't expected her empathy. The heat from her hand warmed him to his soul.

Lately, he'd felt as alone as a man could get. People thought because he'd made millions off the deal he should be satisfied. They didn't understand that the company was more than money. *You got millions,* people would say. *Go sit on the beach or something. What do you have to be upset about?*

She understood. For the first time, he studied Melanie, really studied her. Looked beyond the mayor's remarks. She would know, he thought, because her store was her life, the same way his company had been his.

Maybe that was the problem. He'd been closer to his job than he'd been to his wife.

Oh, crap. Where had *that* come from? Melanie was too distracting. Got him thinking foolish thoughts.

But sitting with Melanie was starting to feel good. He could quickly get used to this.

If it was real.

"With the success of your business, any company will jump to snap you up," she said, yanking him out of his thoughts. Her cell phone rang and she excused herself to answer it.

"What happened?" she asked.

After several *Oh, nos* and *Um-hums,* she pressed the off button.

"Uncle Milton and Elmore are at it again," she said.

"What happened?"

"One of Elmore's boars got out again. I asked Elmore to let the boar use one of the used-up sows instead of sending her off to the slaughter. You see, they use the boars to determine if a sow's in heat. The boar gets stirred up. Being a man, he should understand you can't have a boar to get nature working and then not let him complete the act. How would you feel? They're animals. They have needs. You can't treat them like inanimate objects and expect things to run smoothly."

Melanie motioned for the waitress and Monroe's fork clattered to the table as a wave of passion surged through him. She hadn't actually said that to him, had she?

Trying to restrain the raging desire shooting through him, Monroe cleared his throat. "I'll take you to the farm."

"No, no. Finish your dinner. Your presence will only add fuel to the fire. They're already tense because they're worried you'll sell the plaza. No telling what will happen if I show up with you."

"Just go, then. I'll take care of the bill."

Melanie started to dig into her purse.

"I've got it," Monroe assured her.

For a moment she sat indecisive, but the busy waitress would take forever getting to them.

Melanie left, but the subtle scent of her perfume lingered, enticing him.

It was a long time after she disappeared before Monroe resumed his meal.

As Monroe entered the house, the phone was ringing. He dropped the keys on the counter and retrieved the portable. His heart froze when he heard a familiar voice. Eric Parker. One of his old partners. The old friends hadn't spoken since the hostile buyout.

"Have you forgiven me yet?" Eric asked cautiously.

"Sure." Monroe swallowed his anger. He still felt the betrayal deep in his gut.

"Look. I didn't want to sell out, but after Aaron seduced your wife, we knew that if we kept the company, we'd eventually fold. How could you work together after that kind of betrayal? We couldn't afford to buy him out. The company was worth millions but we were still cash poor. Besides, Aaron wouldn't have sold his share to any of us. He was beyond angry."

Monroe's hand tightened around the phone, and he wished it was Aaron's neck. "Why did you call?"

"Because I don't want to remain your enemy."

"We're not enemies." No. They weren't *any-thing* any longer.

"You treat me like one. I loved that company as much as you did. It hurt like hell to sell. You know good friends are hard to come by. I think I hate that even more. But after you attacked Aaron, I thought you were going to punch his lights out."

"It's yesterday's news," Monroe said. He didn't want to talk about it. "How are Veronica and Sam?"

"Great. Sam asks about you all the time."

Monroe softened. "I miss the little bugger. How's he doing in soccer?" Sam was his godchild, and Monroe missed having the kid around. He and Dorian... He forced the memory away.

"He's a champ. He's the star goalie now."

"Tell him to watch those fingers."

Eric chuckled, then a tense silence emerged. "I saw Aaron the other day." In the silence, he said, "Dorian just had a baby. A little boy."

Monroe stumbled to a seat. He closed his eyes briefly. A baby. The baby he'd wanted.

"You still there?"

Monroe couldn't speak, but could only concentrate on inhaling and exhaling. He cleared his throat. "Yeah."

"I'm sorry, man. I know this is a blow. But I

didn't want you to just run into them. They're coming to visit her parents soon."

"Look. I've got to go. I'll talk to you later." Monroe pressed the Off button, but he couldn't move. Rage poured through him like a speeding freight train. A baby. Gasping to gulp a lungful of breath, he ached as if someone had punched him in the gut. *Damn them. Damn them.*

Dorian had destroyed most of the things he'd valued. His friendships, his company, his marriage. He couldn't forget.

Between desire for Melanie and anger at his ex-wife, Monroe didn't sleep well. He got up cranky and his temper didn't improve by the time he went to pick up Melanie and her daughter for the Blessing on the Lake.

He sipped on his coffee and observed them at the shop while he waited.

"May I get some help, please?" An older woman dressed in a short-sleeved pantsuit stood in front of him.

For a moment he thought she was indicating a salesperson, but she was looking directly at him. He wasn't wearing a name tag.

"May I help you?" he asked.

"I'm looking for a new Christian book. You all sell them, don't you?"

"I'm sure they do." Courtney had just finished helping a customer. Everyone else was still occupied. But she appeared to know the layout. He beckoned her over.

"Hi, Mr. Bedford." She was as perky as someone on a perpetual caffeine high.

"Do you know where the Christian section is?" he asked.

"Over there."

He saw the sign four aisles over. "Could you please show this customer the way?"

"Sure." She graced the woman with a bright smile. "Follow me, ma'am."

The woman followed, visibly admiring Courtney's manners.

Fifteen minutes later, they were on their way to the marina.

Boats tooting their horns lined the lake. Colorful banners flapped in the wind. Every type of food was available. From ham salad to sandwiches to barbecue and seafood. Children ran around yelling and waving pinwheels, and stepping on flowers. A woman on the beautification committee busily scolded them. It seemed every inhabitant of Summer Lake and even more tourists were in attendance. What began as a ceremony to ask for divine protection for those who risked their lives harvesting the lake, quickly blossomed into a popular weekend event.

The vessels lined up to parade past more than a thousand spectators. Three local reverends blessed each decorated boat as they passed before them. A panel of judges including the mayor, the senator, Melanie and the school superintendent rated the decorations.

The crowd was forced to suffer through several speeches. The mayor's was the longest.

Melanie was in her element talking to the minister, members of the city council and hordes of other people. But Monroe always felt out of place around crowds—people in general. He preferred time in the lab alone in the middle of the night when he could work undisturbed.

After the Blessing on the Lake ceremony was completed, Monroe was more than ready to leave. He, Melanie and Courtney hopped in the car and headed toward the rehabilitation center.

"I can't wait to see Mrs. Eudora. I've got a million things to tell her." Courtney was charged up like a battery in the back seat.

"I'm sure you do," Melanie said.

"I took pictures for her. I wish we could develop them first."

"We'll take them to her on your next visit," Melanie assured her. "If you have film left, you can take some of her, too."

"I hadn't thought of that. You can take pictures of both of us."

It was a good thing Courtney talked nonstop because the atmosphere between Monroe and Melanie was tense. He was glad to finally escape the intimate confines of the car.

Courtney was brimming with so much energy she skipped in front of them as they made their way to his grandmother's room.

When she was far enough away, Monroe said, "Please don't mention the sale to Eudora. I don't want her to worry."

"Do you think I'm stupid? I'm not the mayor."

Now he'd ticked her off, but she hid it when she entered the room.

Eudora was sitting on a chair beside the bed, a closed book on her lap. She wore a long blue nightgown covered by her robe. She was gazing into space, but she immediately brightened when she saw them.

"It's been forever since I saw you," Courtney said, dashing across the room. Wrapping her arms around the older woman and hugging her close seemed as natural as breathing.

"Come here, little one," Eudora said. "Tell me what you've been up to."

"I'm getting new riding boots. I saw a pair that was to die for last week."

Eudora looked the girl over. "You look like you've grown a couple inches."

"You just haven't seen me in like forever."

Melanie put a vase of flowers on a table while the two talked.

"I brought you a gift." Courtney handed her a box and sat on the edge of the bed. "And I didn't pay for it out of my allowance. I made my own money to pay for it."

"I'm so proud of you." Eudora slowly unwrapped the small box and opened it to reveal a cross on a gold chain.

It was anybody's guess whether it was real or if it had come out of the five-and-dime, but Eudora exclaimed over it as if it were platinum.

"It's beautiful. Just beautiful. Come give me a hug."

Courtney went eagerly into her arms again, and

Monroe couldn't help thinking that Courtney was the great-granddaughter her natural grandchildren had not provided Eudora. Courtney attached the chain around Eudora's neck and the two huddled together laughing and talking.

"It's time you took jumping lessons. Have you thought of signing her up, Melanie?"

"No."

"It will be easy enough for you to set up a riding rink, Monroe. Courtney should be competing."

"No, Mrs. Eudora. Courtney has enough activities, between 4-H and soccer."

She said it as if she'd go to the ends of the earth before she'd ask a thing of him, Monroe noticed.

"I might not play soccer anymore. Our coach got a new job and he has to drive a long way to work. He can't make it back in time for practice."

While they visited, Melanie straightened the covers and tables. Unobtrusively, she set a book and a small package on the night table. But Monroe took notice. She might be covered from neck to toes, but the pantsuit didn't hide the shape of her luscious curves. Instead of watching his grandmother, he found himself following the outline of Melanie's rounded breasts and gently curved hips, imagining those legs wrapped around his waist.

To get his mind off Melanie, he focused again on his grandmother. He felt like an outsider looking in. It was obvious the women spent lots of time together, and they genuinely adored each other.

Since her family had been absent, Eudora had adopted another. Monroe had never seen her happier. Guilt slapped him. He'd been so wrapped up in his own concerns for the last two years that he hadn't spent enough time with her.

"What's going on in town, Melanie?" Mrs. Eudora asked.

"We had the Blessing on the Lake ceremony today. Reverend Jones asked about you. You were really missed. But I assured him you'll be there next year."

The older woman grunted.

"The summer people are opening their cottages," Melanie continued. "And the stores are packed with college kids."

"And the feud?"

"The same. Nothing's changed there."

"Somebody needs to butt those men's heads together," Eudora said.

"I agree." Melanie finally sat beside Eudora and gathered her hand in hers. "You're looking better."

"I'm doing so-so."

"Are you following the doctor's orders? You can be stubborn."

"I'm ready to go home," Eudora said as if Melanie could make it happen.

"In time."

"I don't know if they have my medication right. I've been feeling peaked."

Melanie glared at Monroe. "Have you spoken to her doctor? How often do you talk to him?"

Monroe tossed a glance at his grandmother. She hadn't said a word about not feeling well. To him or the doctor. "I see him every day."

"I know they want you to walk more. Let me see how well you're doing."

"I do have to go to the restroom." Eudora started to stand and flopped back in the seat.

Melanie hopped up. "Let me help you."

Just the other night, Eudora had nearly taken his head off for trying to help her and had scooted across the floor on her own.

Melanie helped her out of the seat and Eudora moved in halting steps the way she had before her improvements. Melanie frowned after her.

When Eudora closed the door, Melanie said, "Monroe, you may need to speak to the therapist.

She's not doing as well as I expected. Actually she's worse."

His grandmother was a con artist. All this time, he'd thought Melanie was conning her. Perhaps they were conning each other. But it didn't prove Melanie wasn't stealing from her.

They visited for an hour before Monroe took the ladies to dinner and then home. Night had fallen. He escorted them to the door and Courtney disappeared to the back of the house, leaving Melanie and him in the family room.

"We missed Eudora," Melanie said. "Thank you for letting us see her."

"Seeing you helped."

"So many people want to visit her. She's well-respected and loved here."

"I'll speak to her doctor," Monroe said. He was going to have a talk with his grandmother about her acting.

"Please, talk to her therapist. She should be doing better by now."

"She's faking it. She *can* walk better. She'd take my head off if I helped her, yet, she acts helpless around you."

Melanie narrowed her eyes. "Why would she do that?"

"Could it be she wants you around? How can you have so much power over her?" What he really meant was how could she exert so much power over *him?*

Sparks ignited in her eyes. "Power? Simply because I spend time with her? Listen, I've had enough of your criticisms. Get out of my house."

But he couldn't leave. Before his mind had time to register his actions, he'd swept Melanie into his arms and covered her lips with his. For a moment she stood immobile. Then her lips melted beneath his, her body curved against his length. The feel of her lips on his, of softness against him sent shock waves of pleasure through him. He couldn't prevent a deep moan of pleasure.

And then she was pushing at him. Dropping his arms to his sides, he backed up.

"You call me a cheat and you kiss me? Am I supposed to be flattered?"

"Do you think I like this…this attraction that's between us? I know you feel it as much as I do. Let's not play games. You want me as much as I want you."

"I'm not going to do a thing about it. You can't call me dishonest, think negative things about me and expect me to welcome your advances. I don't play that."

"Do you think I like the way you've intrigued me from the moment I met you?"

"I rest my case."

He massaged the tense muscles in his neck and for a moment he studied her intently. Her fiery angry look reminded him of the night she'd hunted him down at his house. He wanted to see her brown eyes gaze with a completely opposite emotion. He wanted the humor, the warmth she'd impaled him with in the hospital. He wanted...

What the heck am I thinking?

"You drive me crazy, you know that? You've got half the people here eating out of your hand." Including him. "How do you do it, Melanie? Do you weave some kind of spell over them?" Before she could respond, he opened the door and disappeared into the night.

He'd totally lost control. She had to be a witch to have him feeling as if he wanted to go back in and haul her into his arms, take her to bed and spend the night there. He wanted to feel her soft curves beneath his body. Crap.

What is she doing to me?

Outside, he welcomed the stark darkness with

only the stars glowing their brilliance above as his companions. Only they witnessed how foolish he felt.

The dewy night air touched his skin and cooled his ardor. He heard the rush of the tides against the lake's shore. He'd just been swept away by the moment. That was it. A momentary aberration. But he lived and worked in a controlled environment. Lack of control wasn't in his nature. Yet, he'd lost it with Melanie. And he hated it. *Damn her.*

He felt as awkward as a teenager. She turned him inside out. How was he ever going to get her out of his system?

Chapter 4

When the door thumped shut behind Monroe, Melanie felt as if an electric shock had blasted through her system. On shaky legs, she fell into a chair and drew in quick breaths.

It had taken a lot for her to maintain her composure in front of him. Feeling breathless from his kiss, she'd almost wilted like a flower in the evening dew. Rubbing her forehead with the palm of her hand, she waited for her heartbeat to settle to a normal rhythm.

Gosh, that man could turn her on like a key in

an ignition. Had her motor started and roaring. The desire shooting through her was sharp and immediate—and strange and, darn it, unwelcome—especially for somebody like him. He called her a cheat, then kissed the living daylights out of her, and she had *the nerve* to respond like some needy featherbrain who couldn't get enough.

At least she'd sent him packing, but not soon enough. Not until after his soft lips had covered hers, not before she'd wanted to hold on to him and never let go.

He must be very satisfied with his performance.

She'd seen the anger in his eyes when she'd thrown him out. But she'd seen something else, too. Was the brief flash of pain in Monroe's eyes before he'd left a figment of her imagination? *Don't be silly. Of course there was no pain.* She was reading him all wrong.

She wasn't about to get tangled with a man who not only distrusted her, but disliked her. She shivered, a chill racing across her skin at the memory of the look he'd given her in the bookstore the week before.

Unfortunately, the memory of that brief kiss crept into her mind just as easily.

She finally left the chair and headed to the

kitchen. At the sink, she wet a paper towel and pressed it against her hot cheeks. It didn't stop the tingling need from raging through her system.

In the last two years Melanie had focused on making a life for her daughter. Any desire, any need was ruthlessly channeled into her work. By the time she'd left her husband, the last thing she'd wanted was another man trying to guide her life. Although she'd been asked out on dates, the drive to get a man just wasn't there—until now. Now, when the most unlikely man turned her on. Go figure.

Enough of that. There was plenty of work to do. Melanie went to the back of the garage to the utility room where the washer and dryer were located. She gathered the clothes she'd left in the dryer that morning, put them on the table and began to fold them.

"Mama?"

"I'm out here in the laundry room."

Courtney came outside, her sour face wreathed in a frown. "We're going to lose another game tomorrow. I don't feel like playing. Do I have to go?"

"You can't let your team down, honey."

"We haven't won any games. It's not that we lose that's so bad, it's that we lose so bad. They won ten zip the last game. We were losing so bad the umpire wouldn't let us play the whole game."

"Honey, things will get better. Trust me. You can't win them all."

Nobody revealed disappointment like a child. Melanie rubbed Courtney's arm, wishing she could do something to help.

Courtney's demeanor changed. "A coach who knows soccer would help."

"Mr. Roberts is doing his best. You should appreciate his generosity."

Courtney looked disgusted. "Mom, you always say good things about people even when they're terrible."

Melanie wasn't feeling favorable things about Monroe right then—or herself for that matter. Fortunately for her, Courtney couldn't read her mind.

"Mr. Roberts gives his time because you girls want to play. You have to be grateful he's willing to coach."

"I should have known better than to talk to you." Courtney stomped back inside.

Well, that went well. Although Melanie had to admit, it had to be daunting when you lost every game as badly as the girls did. But at least the Carson and Hicks girls played together. Well, maybe not together. Their positions had been chosen by the family. Hickses played fullback. Carsons played forward. Melanie shook her head. She wished she knew soccer well enough to coach, and she wished the girls would mingle better. But Joe Roberts wasn't about to breach the feud. The town was too small to support two soccer teams.

Melanie spent the rest of the time she folded clothes thinking about what was really important—not Monroe's lips, or the feel of his arms around her. Not the strength of his warm body pressed against hers, or the aroma of his enticing cologne.

The important issue was how on earth was she going to convince him not to sell the plaza?

But her mind couldn't help tripping to the bleak expression in Monroe's eyes just before he'd left her house. He'd looked so alone, so… She couldn't describe him. She didn't know his story. Only that his wife had left him. She wondered if bitterness had resulted from the divorce. And if the renters at the plaza were paying the price for it.

How should he ever prove how sorry he was? Monday morning, on his way to the lawyer's office located in Summer Lake's tiny excuse of a downtown, Monroe stopped in front of the cut-flower area of the hardware store. The town was too small for a stand-alone flower shop. Tucked in a little corner was a counter and a refrigerated flower case. The gardening area was nearby and hardy perennials and annuals were set out on skids ready for sale.

For the last two nights, Monroe had tossed and turned, thinking of Melanie's soft curves beneath his hands. Tasting the sweetness of her lips was better than chocolate, and memories of those lips had stolen his sleep.

He'd expected to see her in church Sunday, but she'd been suspiciously missing. Coming to a decision, he strolled to the counter where the smiling clerk assured him any flower arrangement he chose would be delivered to Melanie before noon.

With that done, he left and soon entered his grandmother's lawyer's office. The secretary immediately sent him into Trent Townsend's office.

Monroe knew Trent from summers spent at his grandmother's. Monroe had hung out with Trent's older brother, Evan.

"Good to see you, Monroe. You're making a stranger of yourself."

"I wish. Unfortunately, the people here won't let me."

"You were always the loner. Evan had to drag you away from the computer and out of the house when we were kids."

"How are your parents and your brother?"

"Dad's enjoying his retirement, and Evan's got a practice in California. Dad was talking about retiring to Florida until Mom convinced him South Carolina was as far south as she was going. She doesn't want to move away from family."

"I imagine not."

"More likely, she's hoping for grandkids. To her great disappointment, neither of us is married yet."

Marriage was Monroe's least favorite subject, even as Melanie's face popped into his mind.

"So what brings you to my office?"

"I wanted to discuss the rental agreement with Village Square tenants." Even now, when she was cheating his grandmother, he couldn't keep his mind off that woman. Had him hopping to the hardware store for flowers first thing in the morning. He remembered her taste, her scent, the soft texture of her hair and skin. He remembered everything.

"Since your grandmother arranged for your power of attorney a while ago, I can discuss it with you," Trent said, yanking Monroe out of his musings. "Exactly what concerns you?"

Monroe switched gears. "I'm concerned about the amount they pay for monthly rent."

Trent nodded. "They can't afford the actual fee at this point, at least most of them can't. This is a small town, Monroe. Your grandmother felt they would have a better chance of success if she allowed them to pay a reduced fee for the first two years, to give them a chance to get on their feet. I made sure the conditions of the contracts protected your grandmother."

Monroe scrubbed a hand over his head. "Handling the building of the center, and now the maintenance and everything else, is too much for her. Probably gave her the stroke in the first place."

"She never was one to sit still. You know that. If she wasn't involved in the plaza, she'd find something else to stir up. Maybe even run for mayor or something. You should have seen them in the city-council meetings. I thought she was going to attack the mayor." Trent laughed, shaking his head at some image. Monroe could just imagine the show Eudora had put on. "She's just a little wisp of a woman, but she yields a lot of power. I think she frightens the mayor. Are you going to stay a while and help her?"

Monroe nodded. "I want to make sure she's on her feet before I leave."

"Why don't you come to dinner Sunday? Mom has been asking about you."

Monroe stood. He wasn't in the mood to be entertained. "I'll let you know."

Monroe left the office and stopped by the drugstore. Mrs. Seaborn had called him earlier, asking if he would pick up her medication. Her pressure was up, she'd said, and the doctor wanted her to take it easy for a few days. Before she'd hung up, she'd informed him about her swollen ankles, the low-grade headache and several other miseries and ailments. He shook his head. More info than he needed.

When he opened the door, it seemed there were just too many people lolling about for it to be a Monday morning. He made his way to the prescription counter. The druggist hadn't filled the prescription yet, so he perused the card section as he waited.

Now that he'd made a complete fool of himself with Melanie—again—he'd have to apologize for calling her a cheat.

He felt several people gawking at him. He spoke to the ones he knew. The thing he liked most about cities was anonymity. He found the nosy people in small towns hard to take.

"Go over there and invite him to Sunday dinner," Fanny Taylor told her twenty-one-year-old daughter. They were standing near the cold medicine.

Monroe knew exactly who *him* was.

"I am not. Besides, I'm going to be late for class. If Dorian divorced him, then something must be wrong with him. He's old and grouchy."

"Power takes years off a man, girl. And he's rich," Fanny's twin, Flossy, said. "With that kind of money you can put up with a few imperfections."

The Taylor sisters. The only twins in town, and although they were both married, when you saw one, you usually saw the other. Only Fanny had children, but each woman played the mother figure.

"Plus he's mean. He's always scowling."

"Pearl Seaborn says he's okay. She wouldn't lie about a thing like that," Fanny assured her. "She sees him nearly every day."

"His grandfather was a gentle man," Flossy said. "The chip doesn't fall too far from the block. Now, do like we said. Go over there and invite him to dinner."

"I'm not that desperate," the girl said.

"Listen here. I'm going to find you a good man if it's the last thing I do."

Enough already. He couldn't even go to the

drugstore in peace. He couldn't leave this town soon enough.

When the youngster started toward Monroe, he glared at her until she backed up. She cut her eyes at him and marched away.

Something caught Monroe's peripheral vision. Melanie. She frowned at him. With a bag in her hand, she started walking toward him.

"Just stop it. You don't have to frighten her with your bad disposition."

The young woman had hastened over to her mother. The two women and the daughter were now glaring at him. She didn't look frightened to him. She looked as if she'd rather take a crowbar to his skull than speak to him again.

Melanie smiled at them. "Hello. On your way to school, Bridgett?"

Bridgett nodded, but the sisters just glared at Melanie. She turned back to Monroe.

"If you don't want to be around people, why are you here?"

"Picking up medication for Mrs. Seaborn." His sigh was long. "You have a nice dish of crow for me to eat? I seem to always be on your bad list."

"Do I have to cook it or will you?"

"Definitely you."

"And why are you eating crow?" Melanie asked.

"I apologize for saying you cheated my grandmother. I talked to her lawyer."

"Well, good."

"And I apologize for kissing you the other night, although…" All he saw was that *I told you so* smirk on her face. And the V in her blouse showing just a sliver of her breasts, enough to keep his imagination running wild. Her gold necklace dangled just a bit above it. More than anything, he wanted to hold her.

The prettiest velvet brown eyes he'd ever seen met his. "Although what?" she asked.

For a moment he forgot what he was going to say.

He started to say he wanted to kiss her again as much as he had that night, but he shook his head. "Nothing."

The woman at the cash register cleared her throat. "Mr. Bedford?"

Monroe turned to her. "Yes?"

"Mrs. Seaborn's prescription is ready."

"I'll see you later," Melanie said. Monroe paid for the prescription, but by the time he'd done so, the Taylor sisters were bearing down on Melanie.

While Melanie was searching for rubbing alcohol for Courtney's mosquito bites, the sisters cornered her.

"I heard you're spending time with Monroe," Fanny said, her features pinched with concern.

"Are you dating him?" Flossy asked, her hands on her narrow hips.

"No…"

"Good." Fanny nodded and smiled. "Have a good day." Pleased, they marched off toward the daughter.

Melanie wouldn't dare identify the twinge of jealousy she felt at the thought of Monroe dating Fanny's daughter.

"Hum," Melanie heard an unidentified voice mutter just as she was about to go to the cash register. "I don't know why she wants her daughter to marry him. He's as evil as he can be. I wouldn't want my daughter anywhere near him. He thinks just because he's rich he can do anything he wants to. Isn't that right, Melanie?"

Melanie glanced at the woman. "No, I don't believe he's uncaring."

"He's trying to put you out of business. I don't see how you can defend him."

"He's concerned about his grandmother. I really have to go."

Melanie didn't believe in gossip. She headed to the cash register. Although she didn't want her shop sold, she didn't believe for a moment there was a sinister reason for Monroe's selling. Maybe he was cold, but not sinister. He'd truthfully believed his grandmother was being cheated. While she chafed at being called a cheat, she couldn't slander him, either.

Melanie thought of what her daughter had said Saturday night. That she always tried to see the best in people. Maybe she was too forgiving for her own good.

At eleven-thirty, Melanie was helping Gail choose a book for her niece when a woman came into the store carrying a huge vase of gorgeous flowers.

"I had to bring these over myself," she said.

"Who are they for?" Gail asked.

"For Melanie. Mr. Bedford stopped by this morning and picked them out for her. The most expensive arrangement in the store. You have some news to tell us?" She looked at Melanie expectantly.

"No."

Gail's eyebrows climbed high on her forehead. "Do you have something to tell me?"

"No…"

The woman showed no inclination to leave. Melanie got so few flowers, and never any that were delivered to her, that she almost forgot she was supposed to tip. "Just a moment." She disappeared into her office and retrieved some bills from her purse. When she returned, Gail and the woman were still in awe over the flowers. Melanie handed the tip to the woman. She thanked Melanie but still waited expectantly.

"Well, aren't you going to read the card?" she finally asked.

"Yes, later."

"Come on, let's give her some privacy. I'll be back for the book," Gail said, steering the woman toward the door.

With her heart tripping, she opened the card.

Please accept my heartfelt apologies for Saturday night. I hope these make up for my mistake.

The note was signed with Monroe's bold scrawl.

The flowers included a mixture of roses, peonies, lilies and bellflowers, and the arrangement was absolutely gorgeous. What would make Monroe pick out such a lovely display of flowers for a simple apology?

He could have just left it at the apology in the drugstore, but the woman had said he'd stopped by earlier, so Monroe must have already ordered the flowers when she'd seen him.

Her mind wandered to memories of his hands

on her body, and the heat she'd felt. She'd wanted more, wanted him to prolong that kiss. Sending him away had been difficult, nearly impossible. She'd had to pick that fight with him, just to keep from giving in.

Gail rushed back in the store. "So what's going on?" she asked, the door banging behind her.

"I don't know."

Gail glanced at her skeptically. "Is more going on here than I know about?"

"Absolutely not." But Melanie couldn't help her heart melting.

"Anything happen Saturday when he took you to see Mrs. Eudora?"

"No, Gail, and stop asking questions."

"Good thing blacks don't blush, because you certainly look guilty."

"Because you're badgering me."

"Is he trying to court you? Don't do it. Don't do it to save the plaza," Gail muttered. "We'll find a way. Don't sacrifice yourself."

"Oh, for... I am not sacrificing myself. There are limits as to how far even I will go." Melanie couldn't enjoy her flowers with Gail's snooping. She'd had enough. She grabbed Gail by the arm and ushered her out of the store.

"Come by later for those books. Give me a chance to find them."

With that done, Melanie glanced at her flowers again. She started to set them next to a book display, but she expected several people to come tripping in for gossip at any moment. Maybe she should take them to her office. As she was the only one working most of the day, she didn't want the gorgeous blossoms hidden away. Moving the flowers out of sight wasn't going to stop the gossip. She left them right where they were.

Perhaps Monroe wasn't so bad, after all, she thought.

She glanced at the flowers again and her heart was warmed. She picked up the phone and dialed his number to thank him.

When Monroe stopped by the rehabilitation center later that day to see his grandmother, she was hanging up the phone.

"Didn't you coach soccer for Eric's son's team?" she asked, a deep frown marring her features.

"I'm not coaching Courtney's team," Monroe said, knowing exactly where that conversation was headed.

"At least you could help out until they find

someone. While you're here at least. I know you're not staying forever, but you'll be here a little while."

Coaching meant getting involved with the parents as well as the children. No, thank you. "My farm manager is away. I'll have to pitch in more with the alpacas."

"You can't fool an old woman. Anthony's cousin, Jewel, knows more about alpacas than you do. They don't require much work. Besides, Anthony attends conventions all the time when you're away and things run just fine." She tore a slip of paper from a pad. "I have Joe Roberts's number. He has a daughter on the team, too. It won't kill you to pitch in."

He ignored the slip of paper. "How are you feeling today?"

"I'd feel a lot better if I knew Courtney had a coach. Children in sports do better in school. Kids need to keep active to stay out of trouble."

"What kind of trouble can she get into here? Besides, Melanie keeps her eye on the girl. I don't have time to coach—I have to be available for interviews."

"You'll only coach a couple of hours a couple of days a week. You'll have plenty of time left over for job hunting. It's not like you're hurting for money."

Monroe didn't want to be around the town folk.

"I'm about to worry myself to death. Doctor told me if I don't stop stressing…"

"You know how to lay on the guilt. All right, already. But only until the regular coach can take over."

"I'll have Joe call you."

"What happened to your limited visits?" he said, irritated. "People have no business calling you to worry you about soccer, of all things."

"What else do I have to do? I can't stay completely out of the loop."

"Spend more time on physical therapy."

"They work me to death as it is. I've got a torturer for a therapist. I need a break."

"You can take a break when your therapist says you can take a break."

Later that afternoon, Melanie's aunt Thelma tore into the bookstore as if a strong wind were pushing her. "It's been a zoo today," the older woman said. She stopped at the counter and focused on the flowers. "You taking Courtney somewhere on spring break?"

"Can't this year. Too busy." Her aunt already knew that. But any excuse would do to get her in the store.

"Heard you were at the drugstore this morning."

"I got alcohol for Courtney's mosquito bites. I also picked up a card for Mrs. Eudora to lift her spirits. Looks like she's going to miss Easter service this year."

"You're always doing something for that woman. Heard Monroe was talking to you. 'Bout scared poor Fanny out of her wits."

"It doesn't take much to upset Fanny. Where are you going with this, Aunt Thelma?"

She touched a petal on a peony. "Monroe seems to like you. Maybe if you cozy…"

"Don't even think it, because I won't consider it. Besides, he knows we didn't cheat Mrs. Eudora. I'm sure he's going to drop this business about her selling out."

"Never know when something happens to put that notion in his head again. Not good for a man to stay single too long. He gets set in his ways. And just because Dorian was too stupid to know what's good for her, doesn't mean you shouldn't benefit from it. You're a better catch than she was. And if anybody gets him, it might as well be you."

"Thank you for your generosity. Tell you what. Set him up with Gail."

Her aunt scoffed. "They'd be at each other's throats."

"We can't be in the same room without fighting. Besides, he can't stand me."

"That's not what Fanny said."

"What does she know?"

"You're getting a bit snippety, too. You've been without a man too long. I'm going back to work."

Melanie sighed. Underneath Monroe's beastly behavior lay things Melanie had no knowledge of. She felt unnerved by the way something about him tugged deep within her. As if his behavior was the result of some inner turmoil.

Which was exactly where women went wrong. They were always thinking they could fix a man. *He hurt. He lashed out. With my love I could save him.* Melanie was too old to believe that lie. You had no control over another person. You could love them with all your heart, but their lives were the result of what was in their heart, not yours.

A customer arrived. She looked out the window. Several cars were parked at the gas station. One of them was Monroe's. She spotted him looking in the direction of her store as he began to pump gas. Melanie quickly turned away from him and toward her customer.

* * *

Monroe had barely made it in the house before the phone rang. It was Joe Roberts calling to thank him profusely for coaching the girls.

"Just two days a week," Joe said. "If you can't make it to the games, I'll take care of it." He cleared his throat. "Have you ever coached soccer before?"

"I coached a few years."

"Well, if you could coach Tuesdays and Thursdays, it will take a huge load off me. Melanie's the team mother, so I'll call her to get things rolling. I can't tell you how much we appreciate your help."

Monroe grunted.

"You can ride to practice with Melanie. She can show you the location of the practice field."

I don't think so. "Just give me the directions."

Reluctantly, the man did so, then told him he'd stop by later on to talk about the girls' playing positions.

Chapter 5

Melanie and Courtney were almost the first to arrive at practice; Monroe was already there. It was only April, but in South Carolina the day was hot. While Monroe took soccer balls out of a mesh bag, he watched Melanie stride toward him in black shorts that revealed long shapely legs. Her hourglass shape was made even more enticing with a thin blouse tucked into her shorts. He drew in a long breath. It was going to be a long game.

A swift welcoming breeze blew toward him, and instead of cooling his ardor, he smelled the aroma of her perfume wafting in the air. He wanted her even more. Once again he stared at her, transfixed. Her hair was unbound and it shifted in the wind. He wanted to reach out and touch the silky strands.

Monroe cleared his throat and glanced away. "Who's minding the store?"

"Carla Woods, one of my employees." Melanie shuffled papers in her hand. "I have the list of players for you. The addresses and phone numbers are included," she said, handing him a clipboard with all the pertinent information.

Her hand hovered in the air and he lifted an eyebrow. For a moment he wondered what she was waiting for, until he remembered the clipboard. Feeling foolish, he took it from her and mumbled a brisk thanks.

Quickly he looked over the list of names and the positions the girls played. One by one, the girls began to arrive. In fifteen minutes, he started the practice while anxious parents looked on.

First he had the girls do an exercise routine they were unfamiliar with. It was obvious Carsons and Hickses were on the team. The girls Courtney stood with were probably Carsons, so he guessed the girls standing off from them were the Hickses. He quickly jotted down which were which on his clipboard. He didn't want them playing according to the feud.

"Okay, I want you to line up by numbers." The girls moved reluctantly because now they were mixed. He made sure every Carson stood next to a Hicks. Monroe clapped his hands. "Move it. There will be no feud on the field. You're a team. Period." He didn't give a second thought to the parents standing on the sidelines looking outraged.

The Carson parents were standing to one side of the field and the Hickses were standing to the other, divided just the way the kids had been. He noticed that Melanie stood on neutral ground; doing what, he didn't know. She didn't seem to take sides. In the beginning, he'd thought to leave the team in the exact positions their coach had placed them, but the players seemed so mismatched for their positions, he changed the lineup. If the coach didn't like what he did, he could always change it back. But just watching those girls fumble in positions they weren't suited for was enough to make Monroe's stomach roil.

A ray of hope brightened Melanie's day. Maybe having the team play together as a unit would help solve the problem with the feud, at least with the kids.

But one by one, the parents wandered over to Melanie.

"Why is he changing the playing positions?" Elmore asked. "My granddaughter always plays forward."

Melanie shrugged. "I'm not qualified to judge. But Mrs. Eudora said he's coached for several years. So he must know what he's doing."

"He's only going to be coaching a little while. Doesn't make sense he's changing things around."

"They haven't won a game yet. They can't do any worse than they have been doing," Melanie murmured. She met Elmore's irritated black eyes.

"You trust him?"

"He's all we have. Unless you have some other suggestion. He doesn't have to coach the girls. And he's certainly taking the duty seriously."

Elmore grunted and meandered over to the other Hickses. As they huddled, Aunt Thelma approached Melanie.

"Those Hickses always got to be complaining about something, don't they?" she said.

Aunt Thelma was forgetting that the Carsons had come over to complain, too. "Everybody's complaining."

"He's Mrs. Eudora's grandson. We'd best not make him angry."

"If that's the case, we're already in trouble. He's always angry with me."

"Ah. You're just a cream puff. Nobody can get mad at you." She nodded toward Monroe, who was frowning down the field. "Even sourpuss over there."

Melanie swatted a fly away from her face. "The worst that could happen is we'll lose another game."

"The girls are certainly used to that. Would be nice if they won for a change. Good for their self esteem."

Monroe had players pair off and practice drills. Then he worked with players one by one, while the others scrimmaged.

"You must be feeling really good with that pretty bunch of flowers he gave you."

"You're still on that?"

"I don't know what you're so secretive about. It's not like you get them every day."

"Nothing goes on that the whole town doesn't debate, does it?"

"When you get a man like Monroe, it's news."

Melanie started to say he wasn't her man, but after her parting shot, Aunt Thelma rejoined the other Carsons.

Monroe was a hardworking man, Melanie

thought. He put a lot of effort into the girls' practice. They'd never worked out so hard, and after that first set down about the feud, not one of the girls complained. Clearly they sensed he knew what he was doing.

The powerful muscles in Monroe's legs moved with easy grace as he charged up the field to counsel a player. Melanie's skin flushed hot and cold just watching him.

He wore blue shorts and a white T-shirt. The white shirt contrasted starkly with his bronze skin, and his muscles rippling under his shirt quickened her pulse. He put a lot of energy into that game. She wondered if he was as thorough and energetic in bed.

Suddenly he looked at her and Melanie held her breath. His gaze traveled to her mouth, rendering her immobile until he focused on the girls again. Melanie fanned herself with the paper in her hand.

Monroe called the practice to a halt forty-five minutes after the regular practice time. One by one, the girls sidled over to Melanie to complain, but not one word was mentioned to Monroe.

"I'd like to throw in an extra practice this week," Monroe said to the parents. "I realize we can't practice any more during the week, but Friday should work. Any objections?"

Nobody commented. "Good. I'll expect the players here at regular practice time." He focused his gaze on the girls. "I noticed several of you were late. If you plan to play in Sunday's game, be on time." The crowd grew so quiet you could have heard a pin drop. Melanie's phone was going to be ringing off the hook tonight, but now everyone walked slowly to their respective vehicles.

Carsons even parked in a separate area from the Hickses. Melanie had always thought the feud was ridiculous, but never more than that day. She was almost embarrassed to have Monroe looking on. Melanie was packing things in her bag and was getting ready to leave, when Monroe stopped her.

With a towel, he wiped the sweat off his face. "So how many complaints did I get?"

Melanie chuckled. "You don't want to know."

His laughing rumble was deep in his throat. And Melanie realized how much his face changed when he laughed. She'd never seen him laugh before.

"You should do that more often," she said.

He looked at her, a question on his brow. "Do what?" he asked.

"Laugh."

He scowled. Melanie took in the strong lines of his body. Long and powerful. That was a description she hadn't thought of before. He was strong and masculine. *Get your head together, right now.*

"Be interesting to hear your conversations tonight," he said.

"Don't worry. I'll deal with it."

"If anyone has a problem, tell them to call me. My shoulders are big enough to handle it." His shoulders were indeed quite impressive now that he'd called her attention to them.

"I can handle my own problems. I don't hide behind a man."

He looked her over from head to toe.

"I'm still debating whether I'll make you eat crow," Melanie said. "I like the fact that you don't put up with the feud. Perhaps you'll have more success than I did."

Monroe's intense gaze made the hair on the back of her neck stand up.

Melanie's breath caught in her throat. "The flowers were beautiful, and a kind gesture."

Monroe nodded. "I won't lie and say I regret kissing you. I want to kiss you now every bit as much as I wanted to then."

The warmth that stole over Melanie's body was

unbidden and unwanted. It angered her that he could twist her stomach into knots with just a few words.

"Let's get something straight," she said more sharply than she intended. "That's not going to happen again." She grabbed her catchall bag, looped it on her shoulder. "I have to go."

"Running, Melanie?" his voice taunted her from behind.

Turning, Melanie squared her shoulders and faced him once again. "No. I don't run from anything."

With the windows rolled down to catch the fresh breeze, Melanie drove home with only half her mind on the deserted side road. Unfortunately even the cool breeze didn't still the exaggerated beat of her heart. She *was* running. Scampering away from what she felt for Monroe. A man could yank a woman's chains in so many directions she didn't know which way was up. Melanie wasn't ready for an emotional investment. But even as mere acquaintances, Monroe was getting to her. She still wanted him.

"Mama?"

"What, sweetie?" Melanie jerked her mind from Monroe to Courtney.

"I called you twice."

"Must have been daydreaming."

"We practiced harder than ever today."

Melanie smiled at her daughter, who was slumped in the seat beside her. "Good way for you to burn up that excess energy. You'll sleep well tonight."

"I sleep well every night. I don't understand why we can't play our old positions."

"Don't you feel more comfortable in your new position?"

"Yeah. But I don't like sharing halfback with Connie Hicks."

"You girls are a team when you play soccer."

"We're a team as a family."

"Honey, you're part of another team now. You know I don't like the feud, and I don't like your taking sides."

"But family has to stick up for one another. Uncle Milton said so."

"Uncle Milton says too much." How did you explain a feud that didn't make sense to an impressionable nine-year-old who wanted to fit in?

When Melanie pulled into her drive, several cars were already there. The Carsons and some of the other players' parents.

"We'll talk about this later," Melanie said and slid out of the car.

* * *

As Monroe stood in the shower, he wondered what Melanie had meant by "I don't run from anything." Had something happened in her marriage? Had she left her husband because of infidelity? He wondered what her story was.

He ducked his head to let the water splash over him. Maybe he was drawn to her no-nonsense nature. She was obviously a good mother and most of the town respected her.

Just as he soaped his hair with shampoo, his cell phone rang. He assumed it would be his head-hunter with news on the job front. With soap running down his face, he took the call.

It was Veronica Stone, the wife of his ex best friend and partner.

"We miss you, Monroe. Sam's asking about you. How is your grandmother?"

"Improving."

"That's wonderful to hear. Eric and I are trying to arrange a trip to see her. She's a lovely woman."

"She'd love to see you, Ronnie." Melanie reminded him of Ronnie a little. Only, Melanie was a more of a hellion. She might be sweet, but he'd gotten on her bad side. Eric was one lucky son of a gun.

"I called for her address. We sent flowers to the hospital, but I'd like to mail her a package."

"You don't have to do that."

"I know, but we want to."

Monroe knew all the nice touches were from her, but she always included her traitor husband in the conversation.

"Send it here and I'll take it to her." He gave her his address.

"Great. Don't be a stranger now."

"Take care, and tell Sam hello for me."

With chill bumps peppering his skin, Monroe headed back to the shower and rinsed off. His thoughts drifted back to Melanie. Why couldn't he get her off his mind?

It was Sunday and the game was an hour's drive away, leaving the kids barely enough time for Sunday school. The bad thing about traveling soccer was that the games cut into church time, which was a bone of contention with the players' parents and the pastor.

Monroe arrived early to pick up Melanie.

"Where's Courtney?" he asked.

"She's coming with her cousin."

"I can imagine how much sleep she got last night if they had a sleepover."

"Plenty. She slept at home. They met up at church."

"After the game, I'd like her to ride with us. I was planning to stop by the rehabilitation center to see Grandmother. She's been asking about you two."

"I'm looking forward to seeing her."

Their conversation was so stilted, it wasn't hard to figure out that he was still uptight.

Melanie and Monroe were standing together when Joe arrived. Joe had called Melanie Friday night about all the complaints he'd been getting.

Now Monroe had his clipboard in hand and was explaining each play to Joe. Already he knew each girl by name.

"Courtney is good at maneuvering the ball from one end of the field to the next. She's good at setting up for making a goal. She and Connie work well together."

Joe took off his blue Explosion cap, scratched his head, and glanced at Melanie before he spoke. "I don't know about that. With the feud, I try to pair Hickses with Hickses and Carsons with Carsons."

"There can't be a feud on the team," Monroe repeated. "Either they're a team or they aren't."

Monroe was so forceful, Joe seemed to check himself not to take a step back.

Minutes later the girls began to trickle in. Once the game began, Joe made a halfhearted attempt at directing, but early on he gave up and let Monroe take charge. Monroe instructed him on keeping some of the girls on target, while he handled the rest.

Predictably, the Carsons and Hickses stood apart from each other, as if their children were playing on separate teams. But Melanie noticed that halfway through the game, the kids were forgetting about their animosity. They were actually making goals. Not many, but the opposing team wasn't slaughtering them the way they usually did.

Monroe was on them, marching up and down the field, telling them what to do throughout the game. He wore a running suit that molded to him, making him look powerful and fierce. It took some effort for Melanie to concentrate on the game because every time she looked down the field, he was in her line of sight.

By the time he let Courtney take a break, the child was nearly dragging.

"Get a quick drink of water from your water bottle and rest, because you're going back on the field in a couple minutes," he said, his attention never leaving the field.

Courtney sat on the ground. It had rained the night before and her cleats and clothes were grimy with mud and grass stains.

She didn't have long to rest because, before she knew it, Monroe told her to get ready to go back in. She hopped to her feet and waited on the sideline for his signal.

They lost the game five to three, and Melanie was surprised to see the girls so cheerful.

"Good game, good game," one of the parents said to Monroe.

Another clapped him on the shoulder. "Well done."

The girls lined up to touch hands with the opposing team, then they ran to the sidelines for their snacks. For the first time in the year they had been playing together, teammates didn't hover in their own little feud areas. They mingled as if the feud had never existed. For a few glorious moments, Carsons were actually talking with Hickses without fighting.

Joe sidled up to Melanie. "Guess you got your wish."

"What?"

"You always hated the kids feuding."

"It doesn't make sense, Joe."

"Wish he could have some effect on them." He nodded toward the parents.

"I think they may be beyond help."

"Miracles can happen. Look at the game today." It was clear he was proud. His daughter was goalie and stopped several goals.

"Your daughter played very well."

"Thank you. So did Courtney."

Melanie focused her gaze on Monroe as he drank from a bottle of water. He seemed more relaxed around the children than he was around the adults. And although the kids joked with him, it was obvious that they respected him, too.

"Mr. Bedford. If we ever win a game can we pour our drinks over your head?"

"Be my guest," he called out.

The girls squealed and continued to eat their snacks. Parents started gathering their kids up for the long ride home. Monroe talked to the coach from the other team before he joined Melanie. He looped an arm around her shoulder as if it were a natural gesture, and they walked together to his car.

Why was he getting so familiar all of a sudden? He had no idea what an effect his nearness had on

Melanie. The heat from his body burned into her. Every cell in her being came alive. What the heck was going on here? When her eyes lit on her surroundings, she noticed everyone watching them. Was he deliberately trying to get people to think something was between them? If so, why?

"Don't get too close to Mrs. Eudora, Courtney. You're muddy."

"She likes to hug me, Mama."

"I know. But you don't want to get her dirty."

Courtney shrugged.

At the rehabilitation center, while Courtney, wearing her dirty uniform, regaled Eudora with a play-by-play of the game, Monroe watched Melanie. After she'd fiddled around the room, she sat daintily in a chair looking for something to do. It was one of the things he noticed about her. She was always doing something.

The tight jeans fit her curves like a second skin. The neat little blouse had worked its way out of her slacks and she surreptitiously worked it back in.

Knowing very well she didn't like her space invaded, he made sure to stand too close to do just that.

"I knew Monroe would make a wonderful

coach," his grandmother said, breaking his concentration on Melanie.

Monroe grunted.

"He's a great coach, Mrs. Eudora," Melanie assured her.

"Make a great daddy one day, too. He loves children."

Monroe sighed and crossed his arms over his chest. Melanie raised her eyebrows at him. But children had her thinking of sex. She hadn't had any for more than two years. Intimacy with her husband had been nonexistent by the time they'd parted. And she was feeling the loss—especially around Monroe.

Their visit with Eudora was brief, and Melanie hugged her before she left.

"Come here, Courtney. Give me a hug," Mrs. Eudora said.

"Mama said not to. I'm dirty."

"Oh, come here," the woman insisted. Melanie started to tell Courtney not to lean against Mrs. Eudora, but decided not to. Courtney, dirty clothes and all, fell into the older woman's arms, and Eudora didn't seem to mind a sweaty, muddy child wrapped in her arms.

On the drive home, Courtney fell asleep in the back seat.

"I'm starved," Monroe said. "How about dinner out?"

"Okay. Usually I cook before I leave for church, but business was so busy yesterday, I didn't have the energy."

"Do you have to go in today?"

"I have both my workers there. They'll be fine."

When they arrived at the restaurant, many other players were there with their families. Courtney went to eat with her cousins while Monroe and Melanie sat together.

"So how does an obviously successful woman like you end up at a place like this?" he asked.

"Who said I was successful?"

He shrugged. "Just an impression."

"Bruce and I met in college. He finished law school at the end of my junior year, and we got married. Big mistake. I should have waited to get my degree, but Bruce was very persuasive. I had planned to finish my last year, but I got pregnant right away. I never worked outside the home. And it was years later before I finished my degree."

She didn't seem the kind to leave a husband for another man, especially with a child. There weren't any whispers around town of her even dating. And Eudora was trying to set him up with her.

"What happened?"

Melanie was silent for so long, he thought she wasn't going to respond.

"I got tired of my husband's affairs and reached my limit of the way he treated me."

"How did he treat you?"

"As if I was his possession. Our marriage was all about Bruce."

With the way she'd lit into him, Monroe couldn't imagine her taking a secondary role.

"How long were you married?" he asked.

"Eight years. I stayed in it seven years too long."

"Why did you finally leave?"

"I guess it was too many lonely nights at home. I was sick of the women calling for him. Finally, I tried to find a lawyer. But as soon as they found out who my husband was, they wouldn't represent me. He's president of the D.C. bar association."

"Why are you here, Melanie? With your talents you could make it big anywhere. You could work your way up to be a major player in a top corporation. You wouldn't have to get mixed up in this feud. Here, people remember everything, and only give you grief."

"I like the fact that I know my neighbors. The people around me care. I like feeling that I'm part of something. That I'm connected. And that my child can grow up with that connection."

"Does Courtney feel the same way?"

"Maybe not now, because she's new to the area, but she'll adapt. She'll have close ties to family."

"You seem so sure." While Monroe felt stifled.

"I'm not sure about anything. I'm winging it as I go along."

The waitress took their order and they headed toward the salad bar. Melanie got a plate and piled it with lettuce, tomato and cucumber. Monroe's salad was piled high on his plate.

When they returned to their seats, they continued the conversation.

"I think Pearl said you were born here."

"I lived here for ten years before we moved to Chicago," Melanie said. "The slower pace here is great for families with kids."

"Not for you."

"Only because I'm a single mother and I end up running things like the tenants' association and becoming president of the PTA. But I did those things when I was in D.C., so that's nothing new."

"Don't forget you're a soccer mom."

Melanie laughed. "There is that."

"And you look after Eudora. How do you do it all?"

"I don't think about it. I'm fairly organized. It was pretty tough when we were trying to get the plaza going, but now that everything's started, it's easier."

"What was your major in college?"

"Business and marketing."

"How come I'm not surprised?"

Their food arrived and they began to talk about other things.

At one point Monroe noticed people in the restaurant glancing their way, but no one approached them and that was just fine with him. All the stares didn't stop him from taking every opportunity to brush Melanie's hand, to inhale her perfume.

Dinner was drawing to a close, but Monroe wasn't in a hurry for them to part ways. When they got home, Courtney ran into the house while Monroe and Melanie sat on the front step.

Her eyes met his and something deep stirred inside Monroe.

His body went on full alert every time he got near Melanie. He knew he needed to think long and hard before he started something with another woman.

But if he didn't kiss her, he was going to die. He pulled her close to him and took her mouth.

The sweetness of the kiss nearly knocked him off balance.

"Are you going to slap me or send me away?" he asked.

"I'm not going to slap you." Her voice was husky and seductive. "I'm not going to send you away."

"From the moment I met you, I've wanted to hold you in my arms."

He embraced her and kissed her so sweetly it took his breath away. His tongue dueled with hers. He liked the taste and scent of her. His hands roamed over her soft curves, and he knew he was in trouble when he felt her soft hands on him, caressing his neck, his back.

He was always too cautious. But now, he tossed caution to the wind and dragged her onto his lap. Her body curved invitingly into his. He heard a noise in the background and suddenly Melanie was off his lap and sitting at least a foot away from him.

"Mama?"

She cleared her throat. "Yes, honey?"

"I need help with science."

"I'll be right in."

Monroe took a long breath. "Think she saw us?"

"I don't think so."

He gathered Melanie into his arms for one last

quick kiss, then let her go and marched to his car. He knew he was courting disaster, but something told him he had to see this through.

Melanie was sorting laundry and Courtney was in the shower when the phone rang. Another altercation between Milton and Elmore.

She knocked on the bathroom door. "Hurry up and dry off, Courtney. Uncle Milton and Mr. Elmore are at it again."

"Again? I'm tired. Why don't you just let them fight? They're grown."

"Honey, they're old. They might hurt themselves."

In five minutes, Courtney was dressed in jeans and a T-shirt. "I don't have many clothes left, Mama."

"I know, honey. I'll finish the laundry when I get back." Melanie drove the curving roads toward her uncle Milton's. The area was dotted with fields and the occasional house. The aroma of freshly mowed grass wafted into the car. Blooming perennials and annuals brightened the yards. The five miles seemed to fly by, and before Melanie knew it, she was near the farms. Even before she pulled into the path leading to the garden, Melanie smelled the pigs.

"It stinks, Mom. I don't like coming here."

"I know."

"I'm gonna be sick."

"You'll survive. Stay in the car," she told Courtney. If it were up to her, she wouldn't bring Courtney along. She didn't like for her daughter to witness adults arguing.

Melanie sprinted out of the car. Each man was on his own property shouting across the road to the other.

"What is it now?" Melanie asked, stopping between them.

Milton pointed an arm toward an area in his garden where the boar had rooted.

"Look at that mess. I told him to keep his hogs in his pens. He can't have his pigs rooting in my freshly planted garden. He needs better fences."

"I have good fences. The boar gets mean sometimes and plows right through the fence," Elmore said, his thumbs tucked in his suspenders.

Melanie sighed. "Is it the same boar that got out before, Elmore?"

Elmore jerked his head in a nod.

"Have you tried letting him use one of the old sows you're going to sell to the slaughter?"

He shrugged.

"Is there any reason you can't?"

"I guess not. Seems a lot of bother, though."

"Not if it keeps the boar from escaping. Besides, you got no business talking like that around Melanie." He glared at Uncle Milton. "I'll give it a try. Now you give me my boar back. You got no right to keep him."

"You better not come trespassing on my land."

"Uncle Milton, give him his pig, please."

"The next time your boar comes over here, I'm barbecuing it."

"Not yours to barbecue."

Uncle Milton untied the boar from the huge maple and tapped his butt to get him moving across the road. A couple of Elmore's workers took the rope and led the pig back toward the fence. Fighting them every inch, the boar trotted in their wake.

"The kids act better than you two. This feud business has gone on too long."

"The feud will be over when the Hickses give back the land they stole from the Carsons."

"We didn't steal any land. And my father didn't kill your aunt. She fell to her death. It was an accident."

Melanie held up her hand. "Please. They're all dead now. There's nothing we can do about it."

"It ain't over," Uncle Milton said and walked away.

Elmore smiled at her sadly and turned toward his pens.

"Mama? Can we go home now?" Covering her mouth and nose with her hand, Courtney hung out from the open door. "I'm sick."

Chapter 6

It was spring break for the kids, and although Melanie didn't want to impose on Monroe, Courtney desperately wanted to spend time at the Bedford farm with Rainshadow and the alpacas. Melanie thought it would be cruel to keep her in the store all day.

"Let's compromise. If your cousin can keep an eye on you, and if you get Monroe's permission, you can spend the afternoon there. The afternoon. Not the entire day. It's a working ranch, so you can't get in the way."

She held up a hand. "I promise." Poor Courtney was practically bouncing from excitement and Melanie's heart overflowed with love.

"And you have to read a book this week."

"I get to choose?"

"Yes, you get to choose, sweetheart." Melanie hoped she wouldn't regret that agreement. She couldn't take Courtney on a trip, but she wanted her daughter to have special memories of the holiday.

"Okay. I'll call Coach Bedford now."

Melanie nodded and Courtney ran from the room. "Your cereal will be ready when you get back," Melanie called out. "And I want to speak to Mr. Bedford after you talk to him."

Melanie prepared oatmeal while Courtney made the call. Then Courtney brought the phone to Melanie. When Monroe's deep voice came across the line strong and clear, her heartbeat raced.

"It's fine if she spends the day here. I'll call Jewel and have her pick her up on her way in. Rainshadow needs someone to ride her. And we aren't doing anything that she can't be around."

"Thank you. But I was only going to let her stay the afternoon. It's too much for you to have her all day."

"It's really no bother. Let her spend the day. I'll

call Jewel now and you can pick her up on your way home from work."

Melanie hung up. "You have five minutes to eat your oatmeal and fruit, honey. Don't forget to pour yourself a glass of juice."

Courtney sank into a chair and Melanie pulled one out across from her. Courtney was growing up so fast. Her hair was gathered in a ponytail behind her head, but she wouldn't be a little girl much longer. Sometimes it seemed Melanie couldn't keep up. If she blinked, she'd miss an important moment in her daughter's life.

Melanie didn't understand why Courtney's father refused to take a more active role in his daughter's life. She needed the unconditional male acceptance and love that only came from a father. They saw each other once or twice a year, for a day at the most. His calls were infrequent. Melanie had made more of an effort in the beginning, but she gave up when she'd drive to D.C. and he was so wrapped up in his cases he couldn't spare the time for Courtney. It was too much disappointment for the child. Opting out on Courtney's youth was his loss, and unfortunately, Courtney's as well.

Melanie sighed. She could only do so much.

Although she willed things to be different, she couldn't make a grown man change his ways.

Jewel arrived ten minutes later. Melanie kissed Courtney goodbye. The girl couldn't wait to get out of the house.

Melanie cleaned up and headed to the store around eight-thirty.

Around two, when Melanie was taking a break, Aunt Thelma visited the bookstore.

"You and Monroe seem to be getting along well. There's a lot of talk about the game. People are getting restless."

"I don't know why. Monroe's doing a marvelous job. The girls aren't losing as badly as usual. They should be grateful for Monroe's assistance. I know Joe is."

"I am, too. But he doesn't respect the feud, and people don't like a newcomer like him coming into town and changing things."

"Some things need to be changed. You can't hold on to that feud forever."

"One thing you have to learn girl, change is hard. Nearly impossible sometimes."

"I know. Lord knows, I know."

"Your heart's too tender girl. Got to toughen up some. The world ain't pretty."

"When I look at Courtney, I see beauty. I
don't want the next generation to carry that
grudge. I don't want the kids afraid to associate
with each other."

Monroe hung up the phone. He heard Mrs. Pearl
talking. When he marched into the kitchen, she was
wiping down the countertops. The cleaning lady
had already done that. It looked just fine to Monroe,
but Mrs. Pearl always added her special touch.

"Since you're here, would you mind preparing
something for dinner?" he asked her.

She glanced up from the countertop. "You want
me to fix you a steak?"

"I need dinner for three. Courtney and Connie
are coming over." Connie was the other fullback.
He'd invited her over so Courtney would have a
playmate. She was a Hicks, but he could teach
them plays they could work together on the field.

Mrs. Pearl peered at him over the top of her
glasses. "Elmore's granddaughter?"

Monroe nodded.

"I could fix a steak for you, but the kids will
probably settle for a hot dog and homemade fries."

"I'd like a meal for all three."

Pearl plunked a hand on her hip. "It'll just be a

waste. Kids play with food more than anything else. Courtney never eats a whole meal. She snacks. Your grandmother always keeps healthy snacks around for her."

Monroe stopped himself from rolling his eyes. "Okay. It's not for kids."

"Who's coming?"

He should have prepared something himself, but he wasn't much of a cook. In Philly he could always order out. That option wasn't available here. "It's a business meeting."

Cocking her head to the side, she regarded him suspiciously. "What time do you want it?"

"Around five, five-thirty."

"Is Melanie coming?"

"If you need anything I'll be outside." He plunked his hat on his head and escaped. Nosy woman. He drove his truck to the pen where the alpacas were kept. Jewel and Courtney were there. Monroe alighted from the car and strolled to the fence.

As he watched Courtney play with the alpacas, he felt alone to his core. He realized he'd been on his own for two years now. But when he thought about it long enough, he acknowledged he'd been alone for much longer than that. He and Dorian had led very separate lives. Dorian loved to party and shop. Monroe was more the at-home or the one-on-one type.

Dorian was comfortable around people, just as Melanie was. But there the similarities ended. Melanie was generous with her time. Have a problem, go to Melanie. Well, he had a huge problem. He wanted her. His head for her was as deep as the breath of fresh air he inhaled.

"Stop it, Joy." Courtney fed the animal the last tidbit of food. Her voice yanked him out of his reverie. The alpaca followed her around like a puppy.

"I've got to get back to the office, Courtney," Jewel said. "Someone's coming by to look at the sweaters." They sold sweaters, scarves and things made from alpaca fleece on an appointment-only basis. "I can't stay out here all day. Come inside and have a glass of apple juice."

"I'll watch her, Jewel," Monroe murmured. "You can go. When Connie gets here, I'm going over some plays with the girls." He'd called Connie's mother earlier and asked if she could come by for a couple of hours to practice. The offer had been more for a playmate for Courtney than anything else, but he'd used soccer as an excuse. The mother had been thrilled her daughter was getting extra attention.

"You be good," Jewel said to Courtney, rubbing the child's head affectionately.

"I'm always good. Can I ride Rainshadow again?"

"Girl, you're going to ride that horse to death. Ask Mr. Bedford."

"I'll ride with you later," he said. "Maybe Connie can join us."

All was going according to plan. By the time Melanie arrived, dinner would be ready. The three of them would dine together. That was a start.

Monroe felt like a novice. Dinner with Melanie and her daughter. What the heck was he doing?

There was a steady flow of customers throughout the day and Melanie hadn't a moment to spare, even for lunch. She was definitely ready to leave at five. Her assistant was closing that day.

When she arrived at Monroe's, she was told he and Courtney were in the barnyard. Courtney was sitting on Rainshadow, rubbing her neck. Mrs. Claire, Connie's grandmother, was standing at the fence waiting for her. Anthony took Monroe's horse as Monroe walked toward them.

"I want to ride some more," Courtney complained.

"Get off the horse and rub her down," Anthony said. "That's it for the day."

Reluctantly, Courtney dismounted and walked Rainshadow into the barn.

"Evening, ladies."

"I really appreciate you helping Connie with her soccer," Claire said. "She really loves it."

Monroe nodded. "Is it okay if she comes tomorrow afternoon around the same time? Courtney and Joe's daughter will be here."

"Oh, sure. I'm sure her mother won't mind a bit. I'll have her call you later. Thank Mr. Bedford, Connie."

The girl did as she was told, and Claire and Connie left, leaving Monroe and Melanie together at the fence.

"Take a walk with me while we wait for Courtney."

Melanie fell in step and they walked toward the lake. The silence between them was unsettling.

"Did she behave?" Melanie asked.

"She was a perfect angel." Monroe stared out at the water as if he were contemplating the secrets of the universe.

Melanie laughed. "Are you talking about my daughter? *I* think she's an angel, but I'm her mother."

But Monroe wasn't focusing on her words. He was staring at her mouth. The attention unnerved Melanie. She felt her body flame with heat. A swift breeze blew across the lake. Melanie was alert to everything about him. He smelled of cologne and horses.

Monroe traced her cheek with his finger. He bent toward her and touched her lips with a whisper-soft kiss. She felt as if she'd lost her breath. The kiss was so unexpected that Melanie returned it without thought. She liked the taste of him. Before he'd kissed her last Sunday, she had not been kissed in more than two years, but needing Monroe wasn't like needing her husband or any other man. When she was with him, he consumed her mind.

She wound her hands inside his shirt and around his back. It had been so long, so long, that touching a man, kissing a man seemed almost foreign.

"You're like an addictive drug in my system." His breath was warm and moist against her face, and her heart raced. "I can't get enough of you."

Melanie moaned and dropped her face to his chest with a sigh of pleasure, but he cupped her chin in his hand and lifted until her eyes met his. His eyes glowed with tenderness and passion. His lips met hers again, and this time he was far from gentle and searching. He slid his tongue into her mouth and kissed her with a hunger that defied logic and common sense.

His arms encircled her, one hand locked against her spine.

Years of pent-up need exploded within her. She couldn't remember ever being excited like this.

He moaned and kissed her cheek, her neck, leaving her mouth burning with fire. She cupped his head, directed his mouth back to hers.

A swift wind blew against them, bringing them back to reality. Courtney would come out of the barn at any minute. Monroe moaned.

"Dinner's probably ready by now. Will you and Courtney join me?"

"Monroe, this…isn't right."

"It's too late. We have to see where this leads. I can't just walk away from what I feel."

"And what do you feel?"

"A burning ache that won't be appeased."

Melanie shook her head. Monroe captured her lips once more. When they parted, Melanie sensed they weren't alone. Courtney was gaping at them.

Melanie was speechless.

Monroe cleared his throat. "Dinner's ready. I hope you're hungry."

"Mama?" Courtney asked.

"Let's go, honey."

Courtney glanced from Melanie to Monroe, then ran toward the car. Melanie followed her more slowly.

Monroe turned toward the lake to hide the bulge in his pants. The child didn't need that kind of shock. Sighing, he rubbed a hand over his face and waited until his body adjusted before he followed the women.

He kept his distance, far enough away to let them talk privately. He looked on as mother and daughter chatted.

Melanie caught up with Courtney at the truck.

"How could you kiss him?" she asked. "Are you going to marry him? Everybody hates him."

"Do *you* hate him?"

She shrugged. "None of the soccer players hate him."

"Is he mean to you?"

"He's nice to me. That doesn't mean I want you dating him." With a worried frown, she cocked her head to the side. "Are you gonna date him?"

"I don't know." Melanie drew in a deep breath. "I'm thinking about it. Would it be so bad?"

"I have friends whose moms date men other than their dads, but you belong with Dad."

"Honey, I'm not married to your dad anymore." Melanie had tried to shield the child. She didn't want a lot of "uncles" marching in and out of her life.

"I know. And Dad has girlfriends." She glanced at her mother. "Mrs. Eudora wants you to date Mr. Bedford."

"How do you know that?"

"I overheard her talking to someone on the phone."

"I see."

Courtney looked past Melanie, then focused on her. "I guess it's okay—if you date him."

Melanie hugged her. "You're growing up much too fast, you know that?" She kissed Courtney. "I love you."

Monroe watched as Melanie gathered Courtney into her arms and hugged her. The gesture was free and natural. Loving had never been natural to him. His parents hadn't been demonstrative that way.

The following day Melanie relived the heated kiss with Monroe. When they had arrived at

Monroe's house, Mrs. Pearl had still been there. She'd had dinner waiting. Had it not been for her, conversation would have been sparse.

The woman must have known something had occurred. Courtney hadn't been her usual chatty self. And Melanie had had little to say. Only Monroe and Mrs. Pearl had acted as if everything were normal.

"Melanie?" Her uncle Milton barreled into the store just before closing. The last customer had just walked out.

"What is it?"

"You didn't hear? The mayor's bringing somebody around who's interested in buying the plaza."

"What? I thought that was over."

"Evidently not. Thelma just got a call from somebody who talked to his secretary. He's showing the man around town right now."

Monroe Bedford, that traitor. And this after he'd romanced her the night before.

In less than two minutes, Elmore and his wife arrived, along with Aunt Thelma.

"You know what's going on?" Thelma asked, squinting. She wasn't wearing her glasses.

"I don't have a clue," Melanie said.

"You've been spending time with him. Even had dinner last night. I thought you knew something."

Heat of anger and desire splashed across Melanie's face. "We didn't discuss the shopping center."

"Well, what you been doing, girl?" Uncle Milton demanded.

Melanie ignored the question.

The anxious tenants stood in Melanie's store like angry bees, with only the counter protecting her. She talked to them with a calm that belied her inner turmoil. The knot inside her begged for release. These people were looking to her for answers.

As if she had some. She was as baffled as they were.

"What in the world is going on?" Gail asked. Standing shoulder to shoulder, Uncle Milton and Aunt Thelma waited for Melanie's answer, along with the Hicks who owned Hicks Carolina Hams, two doors down.

"This is all news to me. I'll talk to Monroe. I thought he'd given up on selling," Melanie said.

"You set him straight." Elmore put his hat on his head. "It's no telling what the mayor has been saying to Monroe. Look at him coming over here

with his chest all poked out and that oily smile."
Everyone peered out the window.

"Who's that with him?" asked Claire.

"Probably that city slicker who wants to throw us out of our shops." Milton charged angrily to the door.

The mayor was all but bouncing with cheer as he crossed the street, accompanied by a tall man dressed in a navy-blue suit.

"Probably bringing him by to check out the space," Gail said, disgruntled.

Uncle Milton locked the doors to Melanie's Books & Treasures and turned the Closed sign outward just before the mayor reached it. The mayor knocked on the glass, but Uncle Milton raised his fist at them.

"Uncle Milton…"

The men walked away and, after allowing himself a tight smile of satisfaction, Uncle Milton shrugged apologetically at Melanie. "So what if it's two minutes before closing? By my watch, it's a minute after quitting time."

"His first claim to fame is trying to sell Village Square right out from under us!" Elmore yelled loud enough for the people next door to hear.

"Guess we better postpone that trip to New York, Elmore. We got a new grandchild coming in

September," Claire said. "I wanted to spend a couple of weeks there."

Elmore patted his wife's arm. "We'll find a way. I promised Daniel I'd meet him at the farm. See you all later." Daniel was Elmore and Claire's son.

"Are *you* going to run for mayor like Mrs. Bedford asked you to?" Milton asked, his arms crossing his chest as he addressed Melanie. "As long as he's sitting in that office, he's going to be a thorn in our sides."

Gail looked at her beseechingly. "I know you have a million things on your plate, but you could win. Both sides would vote for you."

"I don't have time to be mayor." Melanie felt the beginnings of a tension headache.

Melanie was so angry she left the store as soon as she could. Monroe had taken Courtney to practice. She'd spent the day at his place again.

By the time Melanie arrived at the soccer field, the parents were a somber group.

Monroe knew something was wrong. The parents had begun to loosen up enough to talk to him.

When he saw Melanie, he thought he at least had one friend, but she was as tight-lipped as the others. Courtney kicked her ball around near the car and Melanie waited while everyone else left.

Monroe packed the balls and nets before he approached her.

"What's wrong?" Monroe asked as the last car pulled away. "What did I do?"

"Why didn't you tell me you were still looking for a buyer for the plaza?"

"I'm not."

"Then why was the mayor trotting this investor around town?"

Monroe was beginning to think it was a good thing no one had brought food that day or it more than likely would have been poisoned.

"I haven't a clue."

"He said the man's company was interested in purchasing the plaza."

"Well it's news to me. Although when we first discussed it weeks ago, I never told him not to."

"Why?"

"It wasn't a conscious decision." He leaned against the car. "Melanie, my grandmother is too old to deal with this. She's unwell."

"Monroe, I can take care of whatever needs to be done."

"Which isn't fair to you."

"If you have to sell, at least give us enough time to buy our own units."

"How many years will that take?"

Melanie sighed. It wasn't something they could do in a few months or even a couple of years. They were holding on by a thread as it was.

"There has to be another solution."

"When you come up with it, let me know. Look, I'll try to be fair. I'll make sure the company will let the present tenants stay."

"You can't do that. It's in the lease that we have ninety days to vacate if the plaza is sold. And the mayor's saying these people want to move in brand-name stores, not little mom-and-pop places like ours. We did very well over the holiday. The stores were packed. Sales were great. But it will still take years to break even. All of this will stop if you sell out."

Monroe raked his hands through his hair. "If Grandma doesn't agree, then I can't sell anything."

"You have power of attorney."

"I won't make a decision like that without her approval."

"Promise?"

He nodded.

For the first time since the mayor came by, the burning in her chest began to abate. "Well then, we're okay, because Mrs. Eudora can't stand the mayor. She would never sell to a company he brings in."

"That was when she was well. She isn't any longer."

He tugged her arm, but Melanie moved out of his embrace.

"What is this? Your affection comes with a price?"

She moved closer to him, her head thrust forward. "I don't feel very affectionate when I'm worried about losing my business." Was that what he thought of love? That he had to pay for it? What kind of women had he dated? Melanie had mixed feelings for him, but didn't feel like snuggling in his arms right now. And she wasn't going to pretend.

She sighed deeply. She didn't know what to do but be truthful. "I like you, Monroe. I'm just not in the mood to cozy up with you right now. I'm sorry if it disappoints you. But this isn't just about you and me."

Monroe watched Melanie's back as she hurried away with long, purposeful strides. Courtney was kicking the soccer ball near the car. He wouldn't see her tomorrow. He might as well tell Connie not to come.

He should have known the brief intimate moment he shared with Melanie was too good to be true. For a short while he'd forgotten there was always a price to pay for love. But he'd thought she was special, that Melanie was different. He should have learned his lesson with Dorian.

Since Monroe didn't expect to see Courtney the next morning, he spent an hour checking with the headhunter before he left to visit his grandmother.

"You seem tense today," she muttered. "Are you feeling well?" She was using her cane instead of the walker.

Monroe watched her progress across the floor. "I'm fine."

"Courtney called." Her features grew more animated. "She said you and Melanie are dating." Her smile broadened in approval.

"She's wrong."

Eudora hesitated, blinking with bafflement. "Courtney said she caught you kissing Melanie."

Monroe stifled a curse. "Are there any secrets around this place?"

"Is it a secret?"

"Don't make a big deal out of it."

"I'll be home in another week to ten days. That's what the doctor said this morning."

"It's about time. You're doing well without the walker."

"My physical therapist is a regular drill sergeant. I have to admit he's very good."

"You should tell him that. The doctor said you have to keep up with your therapy after you get home. I bought you a treadmill and stationary bicycle. They're supposed to deliver them Monday."

"I don't like those things. The fresh air is better."

"It'll be too hot soon. You won't want to walk in the heat."

She regarded him closely. "Are you sure everything is all right?"

"Positive."

"You should have brought Courtney with you. She said she was spending the week with you."

"Not today."

"She called me earlier from the barn. She was annoyed because Jewel wouldn't let her ride Rainshadow. And she wouldn't let her bother you."

"Are you sure?"

"I may be old but I'm not crazy. I can follow a conversation."

A glimmer of hope blossomed in Monroe. He'd thought Melanie would keep the child away because she was angry with him. He should have known she wasn't vindictive. Her bleeding heart wouldn't let her curtail her child's joy.

If only—if only she could feel that love for him.

Within minutes, Monroe found himself rushing home. The knowing smirk on his grandmother's face as he'd left irritated the heck out of him.

He yanked his cell phone out of his pocket and toggled to the soccer player's directory to call Joe's house, to ask if his daughter could visit with Courtney after lunch, but his wife said the girl was having lunch with her daddy at the diner. Monroe remembered Melanie's concern that her ex didn't spend time with Courtney, and he was determined to do something about it.

After he reached the farm, he quickly changed clothes.

He found Courtney sitting on the bench watching the alpacas roam around in the pen. Her elbows were planted firmly on her knees. She couldn't look more bored if she tried.

"Hi, sport."

She sat up straight. "Where were you all morning?"

"I visited Eudora."

"I wanted to go." The accusing tone of her voice made Monroe smile.

"I'll take you next time. She's coming home in a few days, anyway. How about lunch at the diner."

She hopped off the seat. "Let me tell Jewel I'm leaving."

In less than a minute, Jewel rushed out of the office. "I don't think it's a good idea for Courtney to leave."

"Call Melanie and tell her she's welcome to join us. Let's go, Courtney."

"But…" When they kept walking, Jewel retreated back into the office.

Melanie didn't join them for lunch. But Monroe and Courtney arrived at the same time as Joe and his daughter, and they got a table together.

After lunch, the men took the girls to the bookstore and bought them gifts. Monroe bought Courtney a butterfly figurine. Melanie didn't want him to pay for it, but he insisted.

He pulled her to the side.

"Still angry at me?" he asked.

"I don't know. What are you doing here?"

"I told Courtney she could pick out a gift."

"You don't have to pay for it."

"Yes, I do. A promise is a promise."

"Is this bribery?"

"No. I decided to take her to lunch when I found out Joe was taking his daughter. We ate together. Courtney enjoyed herself. Anything wrong with that?"

"Why are you doing this?"

"If I'm going to be dating her mother, I have to get to know her, too."

"And what happens when you leave?"

"We aren't anywhere near there yet."

"Mrs. Eudora is coming home soon. You're closer than you think."

"You know Melanie, you can't chart your entire life ahead of time. You try to make everything perfect. But you can't stop living because you don't know what the future will bring. Sometimes you've just got to let go and live." Monroe couldn't believe those words were escaping his lips. Even with her control, Melanie lived more of a life than he did.

"Mr. Bedford?" Courtney called out.

Monroe checked to make sure no one was watching, then quickly kissed Melanie thoroughly enough to make sure she didn't forget him. If the heat wave that washed over his body had half the effect on her, then he knew she wouldn't forget him for a very long time.

"Mr. Bedford?" Courtney called out again. Her voice was nearer this time.

"Duty calls."

Chapter 7

Monroe's kiss stayed with Melanie for a long time. As much as she wanted to banish him from her mind, she couldn't. Although, her time would be better spent devising a plan to save the plaza.

But she'd set aside this day to spend with her daughter and she was determined not to think about work. When she went into Courtney's room, she saw the delicate glass butterfly Monroe had purchased sat in a prominent place on Courtney's dresser. Melanie opened the curtains. Bright sunlight poured in and reflected on the figurine. A prism of brilliant color streamed through it.

"Wake up, sleepyhead."

Courtney groaned, pulling the covers over her head. "It's too early."

"The butterfly is beautiful in the sunlight. Take a look."

Groaning like an old woman, Courtney turned over. Placing her hands behind her head, she stared up at the fragile little keepsake.

Melanie sat beside her on the bed. "Did you enjoy lunch with Monroe?"

"Yeah. I hope we can do it again." Her face scrunched up. "Paula's dad took the whole day off to spend with her."

"What a nice gesture. Just as it was considerate of Monroe to take time out of his day for you."

"How come Dad can't spend time with me?"

Courtney's hair was thick like Melanie's and her scarf always came off during her struggle in sleep through the night. While Melanie gathered her thoughts, she brushed tangles of hair from Courtney's face. "You have to ask him, honey."

"Mr. Roberts went back to the ranch with us. We played soccer for a while. Then we rode horses.

Paula was afraid to go near the alpacas, but I wasn't. They like me."

"They know you. You're over there all the time."

"If it was warmer we could swim. Monroe said if we brought a swimsuit next time we could go in the hot tub. Mrs. Seaborn would watch us."

"Monroe?"

"He said I only have to call him Mr. Bedford if we're playing soccer or in public."

"I see."

"Are we going there today?"

Melanie took the pillow from behind her daughter's head and hit her with it. Courtney squealed.

"You're spending the day with dear old Mom."

Claire had called Melanie to ask if she'd bring her granddaughter Connie over to her shop. Connie's mother had to go in to work an extra shift and couldn't do it herself.

After Melanie stopped by the girl's house, she stopped by to visit Aunt Thelma, who lived nearby. She'd asked Melanie to come by so she could give Courtney a jar of her famous jam.

"We're making strawberry jam. Do you know how to make it?" Thelma asked.

Cooking wasn't Melanie's favorite pastime. She could buy jam from the store. "No."

Aunt Thelma shook her head. "The things girls aren't being taught today. If anything catastrophic happens, most of the country wouldn't know how to survive," she scolded, dumping tons of strawberries into the sink to be washed. "Leave Courtney here so I can teach her. I've got most of my grandkids here to teach them."

"Connie's with us. I was taking her to her grandmother's store. Besides, I'm spending the day with Courtney."

Aunt Thelma frowned at Melanie over her glasses. "I'll call Claire, see if she'd mind her staying."

"I don't know, Aunt Thelma."

"I won't let anything happen to the child."

"All right. And don't forget the tenants' meeting Friday night."

"As if Milton would let me. That man enjoys your stories just as much as the kids." Dressed in their pj's, little kids came into the bookstore on Friday nights to hear Melanie read them a story. This week the tenants' meeting would follow.

So now Melanie had a free afternoon. She got into her car and pulled off. A moment later, her cell phone jingled. She glanced at the number. It was Monroe.

"I hope I can convince you and Courtney to go boating with me. Or if you bring your swimsuits you two can take a dip in the hot tub before dinner. Mrs. Pearl is preparing something special tonight."

"I thought Mrs. Pearl only worked for you once a week."

"With Courtney visiting so often, I asked her to come every day. She makes sure the girls have snacks and things."

"That's so kind of you, but Courtney's at Aunt Thelma's learning how to make strawberry jam."

A beat of silence passed, then Monroe said, "So that means you're free—and alone."

"Yeah, but…"

"Then the two of us will go boating."

"Monroe. Monroe?" He'd already disconnected.

Melanie pressed a hand to her tripping heart. That man! He hadn't given her a chance to respond. He was taking a lot for granted, but a day on the lake sounded a heck of a lot more enticing than going home to vacuum, dust and scrub floors.

As she pointed the car toward Monroe's, Melanie didn't notice the thick forest of trees reaching up like mountains on either side of her. She didn't notice the fields of sprouting peanuts, corn and soybeans. She didn't notice the explosion of flowers in neighbors' yards. But when she arrived at the ranch, she did notice Monroe leaning by his truck parked in his front yard.

Waiting for her.

She stopped beside him, stepped out of her car and smoothed a shaky hand down her jeans. A breeze wafted across her face, bringing the scent of flowers.

He approached her. Was he as nervous as her?

"Mrs. Pearl is preparing a picnic. It should be ready in a few minutes."

Melanie nodded. "It's a nice day for boating."

Time froze when Mrs. Pearl came outside with the basket. She tossed them a smile full of mischief. "I've got a nice basket packed for you."

Annoyed, Monroe took the basket. "Let's go," he said, and he and Melanie fell into step together.

Melanie had expected a kiss hello. Disappointment fluttered through her stomach like the butterflies that quivered through Monroe's flower beds. She'd have plenty of time on the boat to make up for the lapse.

As they boarded the boat, Melanie noticed a

few other vessels bobbing on the distant horizon. But nothing stood out as stark and real as the man beside her.

"Nice boat."

"Oh, this old thing?" Melanie noticed that Monroe's yacht was one of the more impressive ones on the lake.

As they rode in companionable silence, Monroe glanced toward Melanie. She was standing close to him. He was content in feeling the breeze on his face and watching the wind blow the long strands of Melanie's hair.

Finally he had her alone.

With unusual contentment settling over him, he focused on the surroundings. They approached an area that lead to giant cypress trees growing out of a black water swamp. There were no lake houses in this area, only the beauty of nature.

Melanie moved to stand beside Monroe. "This place is so beautiful. We should start a tourist center. The azaleas, camellias and daffodils provide an unforgettable view. They grow a little wild now, but if we want to draw a tourist crowd, we could designate a park here."

The aroma of her perfume drove him crazy. "Who owns the land?"

"It was donated to the town decades ago. Unfortunately, they just never did anything with it."

The flowers were in full bloom. They were close enough to the shoreline to see little dots of color among the greenery. "You want to stop and have breakfast there?"

She laughed. "I don't think so. I don't like sharing my space with the local snakes and other wildlife."

"Then why would tourists want to come?"

"Because it's so beautiful. Look at it."

He did. Cypress trees looming in the background looked almost mystical.

Melanie kissed him. He turned and raked his fingers through her hair. She rubbed his chest and got his blood pumping. He sighed at the wave of pleasure that washed over him. Much too quickly, she left his side and sat nearby.

"Do you fish?" she asked.

"Not really. We fished years ago on summer vacations. Grandma caught more than any of us, even Grandpa. She loved it, but hated to clean them. She always left that to Grandpa and me. Saying it wasn't fair having to clean and cook."

"I like that."

His gaze slid over her. She was relaxed, not rushed as she usually was. "Do you fish?"

"Never been. Courtney goes with Uncle Milton and her cousins. They love to boat."

Suddenly the wind began to pick up. Monroe glanced at the skyline. Not a cloud in the sky. It was interesting the way the water had been so calm one minute and had the boat rocking the next. Monroe steered around and headed toward his favorite spot on the lake.

"I'm ready to eat," he said. "Let's head to shore." His grandfather used to talk about fishing in that spot when he was a child. Remnants of the old dock were still in the ground when the workers built the new one.

When they were docking, Melanie asked, "Isn't this your property?"

He nodded and recognized the two huge rocks he and his granddad used to sit on to fish. This wasn't rocky land. He often wondered how they ended up there.

"You should see the sunsets from here."

"Maybe I will one day."

Monroe stared at her for several seconds. Funny, he'd never had the inclination to bring a woman there before—not even Dorian. Yet he couldn't wait to see the sunset with Melanie. He moved forward, put one hand under her chin, the other around her waist, and drew her close. He felt a tremor pass through her warm body. "There's something magical about sunsets."

"About Summer Lake, too." The breathless timbre of her voice told him she thought he was special, too.

His hand stroked her cheek and he lowered his head. Her lips automatically parted when he kissed her. The long buried hunger inside him instantly flared to life. And when he felt her hands stroke his back, he knew he wasn't alone.

Melanie knew the last place she should be was in Monroe's arms. This whole day had been a huge crazy dream. She knew she should let her mind slide back to reality, but for once she was going to let her body influence her decisions.

She felt his hands run up and down her back and settle on first her hips, then her butt. When he pressed her more tightly against him, she felt the impression of his arousal against her stomach. It seemed a lifetime of pleasure had passed before their mouths parted and he released a deep sigh.

"We missed the sunset," he whispered into her hair.

At that moment, as Melanie tried to catch her breath, the sunset was the last thing on her mind.

* * *

It was late when Melanie and Monroe returned to the house.

Aunt Thelma was hosting a sleepover and had asked if Courtney could spend the night with her cousins. Melanie gave her consent and Monroe eagerly changed their evening plans. She couldn't remember the last time she'd taken a full day just to relax.

The house was empty. Mrs. Pearl had left hors d'oeuvres in the fridge and dinner on the stove— with candles and a vase of peonies she'd gathered from the garden on the table with a note that said *Enjoy*. Underneath she'd drawn a crooked smiley face. That woman didn't know when to quit.

Melanie changed from her jeans and sneakers into a two-piece bathing suit. Then she walked outside on the deck. The pungent odor of chlorine swirled around her.

Monroe had already settled into the hot tub. Wearing nothing but swim trunks, his body hair feathered over his skin with the motion of the jetting water. A bottle of wine chilled in an ice bucket and two filled glasses were placed on a tray behind him.

Monroe leaned forward. His gaze dropped

from her eyes to her shoulders, her breasts and steadily traveled her entire body, sucking the air out of her lungs.

"Come here," he whispered, his voice thick and unsteady.

He held out his hand and she grasped it as she stepped into the hot tub. Sinking to the seat, her insides jangled with excitement. She leaned her head back and enjoyed the feel of the jets lapping water around her. Monroe handed her a glass of wine. She sipped it slowly. The very air around them seemed electrified.

"Enjoy your day?"

"It was the best."

"It's not over yet." Her eyes jerked to his. "Not by a long shot," he whispered.

He took her glass out of her numb fingers and placed both glasses on the deck. Slowly he leaned toward her, giving her a chance to reject him. When she didn't, a featherlight kiss touched her lips. And her already overstimulated body burst into flames. Melanie sighed and wrapped her hands around his neck. He pulled her body close to his until her breasts brushed his chest. Heat rippled under her skin as she recognized the flush of sexual desire she hadn't felt for years. She couldn't disguise her body's reaction.

His hands moved leisurely over her curves and stoked a gently glowing fire. His touch was like a drug, enticing her to give herself to him completely.

Her body ached for his touch.

"I feel…" Her breath caught on a sigh.

"What do you feel?"

Melanie's eyes flew open. "I feel like I've fallen into something I can't control."

"Good. Because I lost all control the moment I met you."

Melanie moaned. She yielded to the searing need that had been building for weeks. His hands came around her, massaging her back, her side. He lifted his body away from her enough to caress her breast. A sigh of desperate need poured from Melanie's lips.

Monroe sat back on the seat and pulled Melanie with him. In a bold move, she straddled his lap.

The feel of her silky skin and tender curves knocked the breath right out of him. Tugging her skimpy top aside, he kissed a waiting brown nipple, arousing a melting sweetness within her. He sucked on it, feeling her fingers clutch his head, guiding him to please her more.

Monroe's mouth on her breasts shot desire through Melanie. Her hands roamed over his back, feeling the texture of the corded muscles beneath her fingers. He took her hand, encouraging her to explore him more intimately. She gathered his fullness in her hand.

"You're beautiful, you know that?"

Melanie's breath caught in her throat. "I want you," she whispered and lowered her mouth to his, sinking her tongue into his mouth, tasting him, suckling on him.

He tore his mouth from her. "I can't wait another moment." Frantically, he reached behind him for the foil packet.

"Came prepared, didn't you?"

"Had to drive two towns away to buy these. Wouldn't dare show up at a counter at the downtown drugstore with this."

Melanie's laugh was full of painful desire. Taking the packet from him, she ripped it open, tossing the foil on the wooden deck and stroked his length as she slid the condom on his magnificence.

And when he slid into her, his tormented groan matched her own. His hands cupped her butt. Skin to skin, they were one. Their bodies were in exquisite harmony with one another. He tangled his hand into her hair, guiding her head down to his for a long unrestrained kiss, until she felt like liquid fire.

Her desire for him overrode anything else as she moved frantically, her pleasure escalating, mounting. He gripped her so hard, she felt as if he were going to plunge through her. But she wanted every centimeter of him inside her. Her breath hitched in her throat; his fingers gripped into her buttocks. She clenched her knees around his waist, and he pushed them farther apart, leaving her more open, more vulnerable. He wanted to imprint his mark on her. He wanted her to surrender to his control. But without conscious knowledge, he realized he was taking as much as he gave. In love there was no control, there was only them; there was only need. And as the blinding flood tide of pleasure consumed him, Melanie cried out as her orgasm shook them both. His mind blanked of everything except the exquisite release that liberated his mind and body. Breathless, they clung to each other.

He was holding his very own sweet southern comfort close to his heart.

Contentment and peace flowed between them. Melanie moved beside Monroe and he gathered her in his arms.

He kissed her shoulder. "Have dinner with me Friday night."

"Can't. I have children's hour at the bookstore and a tenants' meeting following that."

"A tenants' meeting on Friday?"

"Half the town will be there because of their children and grandchildren. We have the children's hour once a month on Friday and every other Saturday at noon. Activities are family affairs here."

"I've noticed. The town doesn't have a movie theater, a skating rink or a Starbucks for the teenagers to hang out at."

"They have to drive anywhere from a half hour to an hour for those things."

Monroe chuckled. "I spent summers here, remember? I'm well aware of that." He curled a strand of Melanie's silky hair around his finger, stroking it between his thumb and forefinger. Feeling mellow, he didn't want to move; he wanted to enjoy Melanie's company longer.

He thought of asking her to spend the night, but some of his workers arrived early and, knowing Mrs. Pearl, the old goat would probably arrive at the crack of dawn to make sure she didn't miss a thing to report back to his grandmother. Wouldn't put it past her to open his bedroom door in the morning just to make sure he was alone. He'd have to fire her on the spot.

So he dragged Melanie to him for one last kiss before they got out of the tub to dry off and dress.

"Melanie?"

"Yeah?"

"Don't worry about losing your store."

"Have you changed your mind about selling?"

"I will buy the plaza from my grandmother. That way she'll be out of the loop and you won't have to worry about providing for Courtney, the others won't have to worry, either."

Melanie pulled back from him as if he'd struck her. "Is this the going rate for sex these days?"

"Do you have to twist everything I do and say the wrong way?"

"No, thank you."

"Okay, maybe my timing was off, but I've…"

He quit talking when she sloshed out of the tub, grabbed a towel and disappeared into the house.

Monroe had been going to mention he'd been thinking about a solution, but that was the best he could come up with. He really wasn't the ogre she thought he was.

So much for trying to do a good deed.

It felt as if a million kids had come for the Friday-night children's hour. Melanie chose

Flossie and the Fox to read to the younger children. Courtney and her cousin bundled nearly twenty children into one cozy corner in the children's book section. Many of the children were dressed in pajamas, with teddy bears tucked into their arms. Even so, hair was combed neatly and faces were freshly scrubbed.

The scene carried Melanie back to when Courtney was very small herself. From their cozy perch on the floor, innocent faces centered on Melanie.

"Have you ever asked your grandmother or grandfather to tell you about the things they did as children?" Several kids said yes.

"Do your grandparents tell you stories about themselves, their sisters and brothers or their parents? Oftentimes your family stories are as fascinating as the stories you read in books.

"Well, Flossie often sat on her grandfather's knee on the front porch with family gathered around. They had no televisions or radios for entertainment, so her grandfather made up tales to tell her."

Melanie began to read the story using gestures and constantly changed the pitch in her voice to reflect different characters. Fascinated, the children's wide eyes followed her every movement. When she was finished, you could hear a pin drop.

Not one eye had fluttered closed. Melanie enjoyed this part of being a bookstore owner most of all.

The adults began to clap, and the children followed suit. Melanie bowed to her audience. Then she began to ask questions, which the children enthusiastically answered. One of the fathers had gotten so involved, he was sitting on the floor with his son, participating as eagerly as his child.

By the time the children left, Uncle Milton and Elmore had arranged seating and a table for the meeting. Melanie locked the door after the last customer left.

Each tenant contributed a snack, for which Melanie was grateful. It was past dinnertime and she was starving. She'd brought drinks.

"I tell you, Melanie, I enjoy those stories as much as the children do," Claire said. "Girl, you should have been an actress. I never seen anybody act out those stories the way you do."

Melanie smiled her thanks, poured herself a glass of soda and piled snacks on her plate.

It was getting late so she quickly started the meeting.

"The way I see it," Elmore said, "somebody has to tell Mrs. Eudora what's going on." He looked directly at Melanie. "She's the only one who can put a stop to this nonsense."

"I've been thinking that maybe we can try to find a buyer who'd be willing to let us keep our space," Melanie offered.

Uncle Milton rubbed the side of his face. "If the buyer decides to sell, we'll end up right back where we are now."

"If only we could afford to buy." Aunt Thelma had forgotten her glasses again and she squinted her eyes nearly closed.

Melanie wouldn't dignify Monroe's offer by telling the tenants, but finding a buyer who would finance them started her mind to think of other possibilities.

"I have a lawyer friend in D.C.," Melanie said. "I'm going to approach him to see if anyone would give us a loan at a reasonable interest rate. You understand the monthly rent would increase if we did that."

"If business this summer keeps up like it has for spring break, we should be able to handle it," Uncle Milton said.

Elmore and Claire nodded their heads in agreement.

"I'll call him first thing tomorrow."

Uncle Milton stood. "Well, Monroe called a practice early tomorrow morning. I better get to bed."

"That man's got a lot of heart with those kids," Elmore grumbled, plunking his Can't Go Wrong with Hicks Hams hat on his head. "Wished he showed that much compassion with us."

Monroe noticed Dorian the moment she arrived at the game. She was holding her baby. A boy wrapped in a blue blanket. Dorian glowed with happiness. She'd never looked that radiant when they were married. Especially in the later years.

"Monroe." The mayor approached him with his hand extended. Absently, Monroe shook the man's hand. "I've heard you're doing great things with our little soccer team."

Monroe nodded. "They're great players."

"You're modest. The poor things hadn't won a game until you took over. Morale was as low as it could get. Your arrival was a blessing for the town."

"They still haven't won," Monroe said. "But they're improving."

"At least they weren't massacred. That's the difference."

Monroe didn't argue. He called the girls to line up for stretches.

"Fenwick was very pleased with the building."

Monroe's attention was divided between the girls, who were taking their time getting in position, and the mayor. "Who?"

"The representative from Fenwick and Baldwin."

With both hands on his hips, Monroe glanced at him. "Who are they?"

"One of the companies interested in buying the plaza. They came a few days ago to look over the town. I gave them a tour. Unfortunately, the shopkeepers were being ornery, as usual. They refused to let us in the stores. You should talk to them about that."

A shadow of annoyance crossed Monroe's face. "Let's go," he called out to the girls, then glanced at the mayor. "You understand we can't promise anything without my grandmother's permission. The plaza is hers, not mine."

"But I thought you were taking over."

"Only up to a point." Monroe watched Melanie as she glared his way. *Great*. Now, he was on her list again. He'd been feeling pretty mellow the last few days. "As a matter of fact, I'd appreciate it if you wouldn't have anyone else view the property until my grandmother is well enough to make a decision about whether she even wants to sell."

"But I thought—"

"Excuse me. I have to get the girls ready for the game."

Melanie kept watching the woman across the way who was sitting with the Hickses. She held a pretty baby on her lap that the other women were clucking over. The woman was beautiful, and looked familiar. Melanie noticed Monroe gazing over there. The jealousy that roared through her like a speeding train competed with her anger at the mayor.

"That's Dorian, Monroe's ex," Gail said in a low vice.

The sidelines were crowded. The townspeople made a family affair of attending the soccer games, whether they had children playing or not. And as far as local entertainment was concerned, the game was the best thing going on a Sunday afternoon.

The mayor's presence at the game was creating a pall over everything.

"He should have stayed home," Melanie snapped, gazing at the mayor. Her cousin turned to see whom she was talking about.

"What's he doing here, anyway?"

"Came to gloat." He'd clapped Monroe on the back when he'd arrived and spoken with him a couple of minutes before cruising the sideline like someone important. Then Melanie heard a rumble come up the line, starting with the Hickses.

She glanced around. "What's going on?"

"I don't know." Gail left to speak with her mother, who was always up-to-date on the latest news.

A huge cheer rent the air and everyone on the Lake Explosion side started clapping. Monroe glanced at her with a question on his brow. Melanie shrugged.

In a couple of minutes, Gail sprinted back to Melanie, a huge grin splitting her face.

She immediately hugged Melanie. "Girl, why didn't you tell me? It's about time. Just tell me what to do. I'll help you."

Baffled, Melanie looked at Gail as if she were crazy. "What are you talking about?"

Gail rolled her eyes. "You're running for mayor. That's what everyone was cheering about."

"What?" Melanie glanced around and sure enough everybody was grinning and started clapping again—Hickses and Carsons alike.

"That's what Mama told me. You're going to have to get a campaign manager. We'll all pitch in for expenses. We don't expect you to carry the burden alone. That's what fund-raising is for."

Melanie hadn't given the political position a thought. As if she really had the time to run for office. But everyone had been depressed over the buyers the mayor kept canvassing. Obviously, he hadn't heard the false rumor because he stood near Monroe with that same self-important smirk on his face.

Instead of doing something to help the community, he was trying to tear down the two years of hard work they'd put into the plaza.

Melanie didn't have the heart to correct the others. She'd have to sleep on it.

"I feel so much better. He's going to have his work cut out for him. If he wants even a fighting chance, he won't have time to search out prospective buyers."

Melanie glanced around. The shop owners were sitting straighter in their seats. The ones standing were standing tall.

She focused on Monroe. The players were hovered together and he was giving them instructions. They had yet to win a game. But on the last game, the score was tied. The extra time they'd put in for individual training was already apparent.

It was almost as if Monroe were two people. He could be so kind, yet he had the power to pull the rug out from under their feet.

How on earth could she let these people down?

* * *

The Explosion won their game. The girls were so joyful, Monroe had to remind them to shake hands with the opposing team. They hopped into line and completed the duty before they raced back to the sidelines jumping and screaming.

Monroe gave the girls a moment to enjoy their victory before he talked to them. Courtney nearly bowled him over when she launched herself into his arms for a hug.

Monroe stood in place, clearly stunned.

"Thank you, thank you, thank you." Then she raced back to her friends as if it had never happened.

"You okay?" Melanie asked.

"Sure." But he was clearly touched.

"She can be a little overwhelming if you aren't used to her."

"I've noticed."

The girls huddled together. Then as one they ran to Monroe and tossed their drinks over his head. Melanie moved back so she wouldn't be soaked as well.

The parents laughed at his reaction.

"Mama, can I go home with Aunt Thelma? Uncle Milton's going to start the grill. We're having a cookout."

"All the kids are coming over," Aunt Thelma said. "We'll drop them off at home later on. You don't have to pick 'em up."

"All of them?"

Aunt Thelma turned and started to walk away. "Wouldn't be right otherwise."

"All right," Melanie said.

Uncle Milton drove one van and his son drove the other. Hickses and Carsons scrambled into one vehicle or the other in a jumble.

"I can't believe it," Monroe said as the cars disappeared in a cloud of dust and he dried himself off with a towel.

Melanie shook her head. Neither could she.

People started leaving until only a handful remained. They started carrying things to the car. A few yards away Melanie noticed two teens bickering. One was a Carson. The other a Hicks, of course. Before Monroe could approach them, they were punching at each other.

Monroe ran to them, and pulled them apart, but they were still swinging. Before he knew it, there was a gash on his arm and someone had popped him upside the head.

"Quit it!"

They stopped as if stunned. "Sorry, Mr. Bedford. Didn't mean to hit you."

"Well you did. And this is the last game you'll attend. Stay away until you learn how to act. Both of you. Now go."

"I'm ashamed of you, Marcus Carson," Melanie said. "What's gotten into you? And you too, Roger Hicks. What's the matter with you? Go home right now!"

"Sorry, Melanie."

"Sorry doesn't cut it."

Looking sheepish, the boys got into their respective cars and drove away.

With the dust settling in the air, Melanie saw Monroe's arm for the first time. "You're bleeding. I've got some bandages."

She rushed to the first-aid bag she kept on hand for the games and took out wipes and bandages. "Here, sit on the bench."

Melanie tore open the antiseptic package and swabbed the cut before she bandaged it. Monroe didn't utter a whimper as she worked with fingers that felt like all thumbs. By now they were alone in the park, and Melanie felt the isolation.

Monroe wrapped his hands around her waist

and kissed her stomach. She felt the heat of his breath through her wispy blouse.

The desire that rocked through Melanie startled her. She lifted a hand and rubbed his shoulders, his head.

He pulled her down until she was sitting on his lap and he guided her mouth to his, kissing her deeply. Feeling warm and aroused, she returned his kiss with equal fervor.

"I must be out of my mind," Melanie said when she came up for breath.

"Why?"

"There's just too many things unsettled between us and I've gone to bed with you."

"The plaza."

"That and the fact that you're on the rebound."

"Dorian and I have been divorced long enough for me to move on. Aren't you ready for something more?"

"But you still have feelings for her."

"You know, I thought I was still angry with her, but today when I saw her, I didn't feel anything. I didn't feel anger, hurt, love. It's over. As for the plaza, my grandmother is too old to handle the units."

"It's more than that." Melanie looped her arms around his neck and settled close to him. "Don't you realize she needs the plaza? Making a difference helps her feel useful. It gives her life purpose. Regardless of how old you are, you still need a reason for being. The plaza gives her a reason to get up every day. She does very little anyway. She comes to my shop almost daily. Not to work, but because she needs to be around people—people who care.

"Besides, if the plaza is a problem, I'll be more than willing to handle it. Except she isn't going to let me take it over completely. Because it's her baby."

"I don't want to talk about the plaza, Melanie. I just want you." He brought her head to his once more and kissed her.

"Have dinner with me," he said minutes later.

"I cooked this morning. Have dinner with me."

"Okay."

The inside of his car was charged with need and expectation as they drove home.

Monroe reached across the seat and gathered Melanie's hand in his. Bringing it to his lips, he planted a warm kiss.

Melanie was still peeved over his offer to buy the plaza, but maybe she was putting too much into it. She wasn't willing to cross that line between business and lover, even though he might be willing to.

Chapter 8

It took Melanie more than a week to reach Gregory, her lawyer friend from D.C.

"You know, you wouldn't have a thing to worry about if you just married me," he said half joking, half serious.

"I couldn't do that to a dear friend."

"A woman of morals. You're a rare breed."

"You only feel that way because you date the wrong kind of women."

"If she's a looker, she's the right kind."

"One day, is all I have to say," Melanie said,

wishing he dated more serious women, the kind who wanted him for the tender man beneath the bold exterior. One who really loved him.

"Well, since you won't have me, I have to settle for the next best thing."

"That's just a convenient excuse. I hate to ask more of you. Not after everything you've done for me." He'd been the only lawyer willing to take on her divorce case even though that wasn't his forte. Had it not been for him, she and Courtney would have been left nearly destitute. Her ex would have turned over any stone to hold on to all the money, as if the thousands of meals she'd cooked over the years meant nothing, along with the floors she'd scrubbed and the bathrooms she'd cleaned before they could afford a housekeeper. As if the professional functions she'd overseen didn't count. As if the nights of helping their daughter with homework, taking her to extracurricular activities, functioning as PTA president, helping out in school and caring for their home were inconsequential. And she would have lost custody of Courtney, even though her ex had spent little time with the child, even when they'd lived under the same roof. Even though her house wasn't as grand as their home in D.C. had been, Gregory had made it possible for her to pay for her house in cash, cruise out of town in her Cadillac SRX and thumb her nose at the SOB on her way.

"You can ask me anything, you know that," Gregory was saying.

She explained her situation to him.

"I know a few investors who might be willing to take on the loan. First, put together a business plan and we'll go from there."

"Thanks, Gregory."

"Anytime, sweetheart."

Slowly Melanie hung up the phone, relief spreading through her. If Gregory said he would help, it was as good as done. She couldn't wait to tell the other tenants. That'd really stick in the mayor's craw.

"Grandma, I want you to move into my house while you recuperate," Monroe said. "I have a room already set up for you." He tossed her plastic pitcher into a box. She'd accumulated so much stuff while at the hospital, he should have brought the truck.

"I'm going to my own house," she said, with a stubborn tilt to her chin. "I miss it." She folded some slacks neatly and piled them on top of a stack in her suitcase.

"I have a downstairs bedroom. You won't have to climb stairs."

"So do I."

Monroe sighed. "Fine. If you refuse to stay with me, I'll move into your house." The older she got, the more difficult she became.

"No, you won't."

Monroe struggled with annoyance. "You've got to fight about everything, don't you? Why don't you listen to reason? You can't stay alone. I won't have it. Either you move in with me or I'm moving in with you. Period."

"I will box your ears. Don't think you're too old."

Monroe glanced at the little scrap of a woman.

"I've already hired someone," she said, her chin tilted with defiance. "Pearl's going to stay with me for as long as I need her."

"She runs a cleaning business. You'll be alone during the day."

"Those girls know how to clean by now. She's just in the way with nothing else to do but bug people. She can take care of her paperwork at my place." She snapped the suitcase closed. "My things are all packed. I'm ready to go home."

"As soon as I pack the car, I'll come back for you." Monroe gathered her suitcase and one of the

bags. Between thoughts of Melanie and his grandmother, his temper was quickly rising.

Maybe having Mrs. Seaborn occupied with his
grandmother would keep the housekeeper from
butting into his affairs. Maybe he could have
Melanie over to his house without worrying about
his business spreading all over town. Not that he
was trying to keep her a secret. He just wasn't
used to people meddling in his affairs.

Although he dated Melanie, unofficially anyway,
she still hadn't completely forgiven him for offering
to buy the plaza. She flat out refused to discuss it
with him under any terms. Why couldn't she
believe that he had a heart? That he didn't want to
put all those people out of business? But just like
his grandmother, she was a stubborn woman. He
was destined to be surrounded by them.

In the face of her unbending nature, he had no
option but to let the plaza rest—for now.

Mrs. Eudora was coming home. Melanie
arranged the party with Mrs. Pearl's help. The older
woman came over the day before to supervise the
cleaning and move her things into a spare bedroom.

The shopkeepers from the plaza all contributed
something for the party. Melanie, her aunt Thelma,

Claire and Gail set up Mrs. Eudora's dining-room table with the food and drinks. Melanie contributed Mrs. Eudora's special peach pie. The aroma from Aunt Thelma's hot yeast rolls were so tempting, Melanie wanted to slather them with butter and eat a dozen, but she'd only eaten one—so far. Thanks to her aunt's great cooking, Melanie's waistline was already thickening and her jeans were hugging her hips a little too tightly. And she didn't have the money to buy a new wardrobe, especially since the future of her business was still up in the air.

The one person they didn't invite was the mayor.

"That's the strawberry jam the kids made," Aunt Thelma said, dishing the jam into a colorful bowl. "Seeing as how much she's taken with little Courtney, I thought she'd appreciate it. I've got a whole jar just for her in that basket over there." Aunt Thelma and Claire had made up a basket of goodies from the proprietors. Melanie had contributed romance and thriller novels.

"I'm sure she will enjoy it." Melanie had to admit the jam came out very well. Maybe she should have sat in with the kids. But the thought of Monroe and her making love that night had her face heating up.

"It is pretty warm in here. Maybe we should get Pearl to turn the air-conditioning up."

"I'm all right. No need to do that."

"Melanie," Aunt Thelma said, dishing a jar of watermelon pickles into a dish. "You've got to start your campaign right away."

"My decision isn't signed in stone yet."

"I know. But if you're going to do it, you're going to have to announce it soon, and in church. Andrew has been the mayor so long, most people don't go to the polls any longer. We've got to get people interested. Got to get them motivated to make the effort. Jobs speak to people's heart. They already know the mayor's gonna do nothing. But he's a fast talker. He'll talk up this company like they have the community's interest at heart. But the only thing I see coming is low wages and no benefits. We need something bigger to hoist the town up."

"That's for sure. I wish I could pull a large company in. It would keep the young college graduates in town and draw more customers for the stores, not only ours but others in town. Jobs keep a town growing."

"You see? We need young blood to stir things up, to keep us from stagnating. Andrew's been the mayor too long. He's gotten lazy with the job. He was always lazy."

"You're determined to make me run, aren't you?"

"You're right about that. And while we're on the subject of the mayor, I heard it was a long time before you got home after the game. After the boys started throwing punches, you and Monroe were the only ones left at the park. What took you so long to leave?"

"If we were the only ones there, how do you know how long it took us to leave?"

"You've got to pass by Fanny's house. She likes to look out the window to see who's driving by. And she knew exactly when Monroe's car drove by with you sitting in the passenger seat. What were you doing out there?"

"Monroe got scraped when he broke up the fight. I had to bandage him up."

Her aunt gave her a narrow look. "Took that long to put on a bandage? Christ, child I could bandage a knee and keep on trucking. Maybe you were bandaging up that broken heart of his."

"I think his heart's mended."

"You know I never cared that much for the Hickses, but I never had much against them, either. It's Milton who won't let the past go. But what that gal did to Monroe was pure dirty. Some people have no couth. She knew Monroe was here and she goes sporting that baby about like a trophy or something. He's got to feel mighty bad to lose his wife the way he did. So if you did stay behind to pet him up a little, I don't see any harm done."

"You won't leave it alone, will you?"

"Girl, you think I don't see the spark in your eyes when he comes around? And you don't think I see him 'bout to break his neck to watch you when you're around him? I'm not the only one noticing things. And it's got nothing to do with the plaza." Her aunt smiled. "Fanny is some kind of angry with you. She had her heart set on getting him for her son-in-law."

"What're you all whispering about over here?" Gail asked.

"Your cousin and her new beau."

"Oh, that. If you don't intervene, it might take you a couple of years to get him to the altar," Gail said.

"He's not that slow, girl. Believe me," Aunt Thelma said. "He's making his moves."

Melanie couldn't stop the heat from seeping to her face. She hoped it didn't show. Aunt Thelma had her eye on everything. Nothing skipped her observation.

"As hard as you work, how do you keep up with all the news?" she asked the older woman.

"If I could only do one thing at a time, I'd be in big trouble."

Melanie was grateful Aunt Thelma had kept her radar hidden the evening she and Monroe had made love. The intense feelings she felt that night were new and exciting. That deep, piercing need and complete satisfaction had been missing with her ex. Probably because he was too busy spreading his joy to too many administrative assistants looking for raises. Contrary to what some men thought, they couldn't give their all to more than one woman.

And then Monroe had had to go and ruin it with his offer to buy the shopping plaza.

"Hide, hide!" Melanie jumped a foot. Claire came bustling in, yanking Melanie out of her amorous thoughts.

Only a couple of cars were parked outside to ensure the party would stay a surprise. The men were due to arrive ten minutes after Mrs. Eudora. Monroe was supposed to call Uncle Milton, and he was going to tell the others.

"They're coming up the lane," Claire shouted. "Cut the lights."

"You gonna give her a heart attack if you jump out at her. We'll stand near the door so she'll see us as soon as she comes in," Aunt Thelma added.

Claire hustled the kids up from their perch in front of the TV in the family room. She'd worked herself into such a state, the poor woman was winded by the time Mrs. Eudora appeared at the door.

Despite Aunt Thelma's warning, seeing so many people in her house still shocked the older woman speechless.

"Well, I never expected this." It was clear Mrs. Eudora was pleased. Very pleased.

Courtney ran to her and hugged her, then dragged Mrs. Eudora's purse out of her hand.

"Put it on my bed, sweetie," she whispered in her ear while hugging the child. When Courtney skipped away, Mrs. Eudora moved farther into the room. Even though her smile was bright, she fairly drooped with fatigue. Taking charge, Aunt Thelma steered her to a comfortable wingback chair in the living room.

"I know you're hungry," Aunt Thelma said, fussing over her. "I'll fix you a plate."

"I could use a bite to eat. Haven't had a decent meal since I left here." She shook her head. "Seems as though I've been gone forever. It sure is good to be home." She looked around the room as if she couldn't believe she was back. She was clearly overwhelmed. She rubbed the armrest. Things looked as they had when she'd left.

"Now, now. I kept things dusted and cleaned," Mrs. Pearl assured her, tossing a narrow look at Aunt Thelma's back. Mrs. Pearl didn't like anybody taking over what she considered her territory.

Aunt Thelma returned with a plate heaping with enough food to satisfy a linebacker, and a warm damp washcloth for Mrs. Eudora to wash her hands with. After Mrs. Eudora wiped her hands, she took the plate.

"I missed good food most of all," she said. "I've had enough bland food to last a lifetime. It was awfully nice for you all to welcome me home."

"I only brought you a small piece of ham. I know you can't eat much pork. But it's as delicious as always."

As Mrs. Eudora gloried in being woman of the hour, Melanie glanced across the room. Her gaze set on Monroe's. He shut his cell phone and his gaze caressed her with its warmth and promise of intimacy and heat. Everything faded around her except him. Her body ached for his touch again. Things were different now. Before she hadn't

known what she was missing. Now that she'd
sampled intense pleasure from him, volcanic heat
spread through her body. She wanted him with
each breath that she took. When a tender smile
spread across his lips, she nearly spilled her glass
of punch. She wanted to reach out to him; she
yearned to walk into his welcoming embrace.

Melanie tore her gaze away. "I…I'm going to
put your punch on the table." With a trembling
hand, Melanie placed the glass on the coaster. Mrs.
Eudora looked sharply at her, then at Monroe,
whom Mrs. Pearl had engaged in a conversation,
and smiled. Melanie couldn't meet the woman's
eyes, fearing their intimate encounter was printed
all over her face.

Mrs. Eudora reached out and touched her hand
tenderly. "It's okay. You've made me the happiest
woman in the world. I've never seen him so
content," she whispered in Melanie's ear.

Melanie closed her eyes briefly because she
couldn't envision a future with Monroe. She
loathed granting this kind and loving woman false
hope, only to disappoint her. Convenient words
trapped themselves in her throat. There was
nothing she could say.

Boisterous laughter preceded Uncle Milton,

Elmore and other men as they appeared through the door and headed to Mrs. Eudora, giving Melanie the opportunity to escape the woman's knowing gaze. But Melanie couldn't escape her feelings. After briefly speaking to the older woman, the men headed straight to the buffet.

Mrs. Eudora thought Melanie was the catalyst that would keep Monroe in town, but Melanie knew she didn't possess that kind of control over him.

Every time Melanie looked up, Monroe was entertaining guests. God, he was such a striking man. Even more, he didn't recognize his potency. It was a natural part of him. At the rate he was going, he would starve before he made it to the buffet table. Melanie fixed him a plate and handed it to him.

"Eat."

He chuckled. "How did you know I was famished? Thank you, sweetheart."

His voice whispered over her skin like a caress. *Sweetheart?* The moment was lost when someone new engaged him in conversation.

Mrs. Eudora tired easily, so the party was in full swing when Melanie led the older woman to her room for some peace and a nap. As soon as her head touched the pillow, Melanie turned the lights out and quietly left the room.

"Melanie needs a campaign manager. You know anyone capable of the job?" Gail asked her father, who was talking to Monroe.

"Heck girl, we're going to tell everybody near and far. Won't need any banners and flyers. People are going to know."

Gail shook her head. "She needs a campaign manager, Dad. You know the mayor is going all out. She can't do less."

"We're all going to be campaigning for her. Whatever she wants is okay with me."

Monroe noticed that even at his grandmother's party, except for Claire and Thelma, the Hickses and Carsons pretty much stayed with their own groups. The women had obviously built an alliance while working next door to each other.

Monroe sat in the soft chair by his grandmother's bed.

"Welcome home," he said.

"Glad to be here. And the party. Seeing everyone after so long. It was wonderful."

"Not that you'd listen to me, but I think you overdid it on your first day." Most of the people had left. Melanie and some of the ladies had remained behind to help Mrs. Pearl clean up.

"I'll leave you so you can rest some more."

She reached out and touched his hand. "Sit with me for a little while."

Monroe settled back in the chair. Knowing very well Mrs. Pearl had regaled his grandmother with his and Melanie's romance, he waited for the questions.

"Have you thought about building that rink for Courtney? She loves to ride and she's very good. Competing would be good for her. It will open her up for different experiences."

"I'll consider it."

"Jobs are pretty hard to come by around here. People could use the money."

"Is that why you built the plaza?"

She patted the pillow behind her and moved to a more comfortable position.

"I had selfish reasons, too. I'd become complacent. Your grandfather and I were very active. We were always involved in things. We were leaders in the community." Her eyes grew misty as she gazed at the photo of the tall, striking man on her bedside table.

"I was lucky, Monroe." Her voice was as tender as her gaze. "I married the man I loved. At my age I never expected to find that again. Darn lucky to find it the first time. What we shared gives me the courage and strength to go on without him."

She lifted her gaze to Monroe with the eyes of a woman who'd been thoroughly loved and who loved in return. It took a powerful and humble man to make a woman remember him that way. Monroe wished some of what his grandfather had had ran through his own veins. Instead he'd messed up things with Melanie before they'd started.

"But my life was running on empty—until Melanie came along. She charged into town like a hurricane, all excited and pumping everybody up. You should have seen her in those council meetings. Standing tall and proud, talking with a sophistication and knowledge that had everybody eating out of her hand."

"Except the mayor."

She fanned a dismissive hand. "Oh, that old fool. I said to myself then, the town needs her. It needs somebody to shake them up. The people who run the shopping center need her. There aren't enough jobs here. She could really do the residents of Summer Lake some good."

Monroe bent and kissed his grandmother's wrinkled cheek. "Good night. I'll be back in the morning."

She winked at him. "You and Melanie look great together."

Monroe rolled his eyes. "You're never going to give up on that, are you?"

Eudora shrugged and yawned. "Just an observation."

Closing the bedroom door, Monroe joined Melanie in the kitchen. She and Thelma were helping Mrs. Pearl put away the last of the serving platters.

"I'm plumb ready for bed," the older woman said. "What a nice party."

Uncle Milton came in the back door. "I put all your dishes in the car, Thelma." He tapped her on the backside, eliciting a yelp. Her cheeks actually heated up.

"You're too old to be doing that, especially in front of the young folks."

"Speak for yourself, woman. I'm not too old for anything. Let's hustle." Uncle Milton looked like a man ready to toss his wife onto the bed. "Melanie, I'll drop you off."

"Don't worry about it. I'll drop Melanie off on my way home," Monroe muttered quickly. "Ready?"

"Let me get Courtney and grab my purse."

"Thanks, Mrs. Pearl," Monroe called out.

"Oh, any time. Come on by in the morning. I'll have a nice breakfast cooked up."

And an ear waiting to soak up gossip.

When Monroe returned home, the light was flashing on his answering machine. He depressed the Play button. The message was from someone at Emerson, the company that had bought out his company. His mouth tightened in irritation. He'd return the call in the morning.

Not fifteen minutes had passed when the phone rang again. It was the president of Emerson asking him to head the engineering team of a subsidiary they wanted to build in Pennsylvania. Aparently they wanted to manufacture a product Monroe had convinced his partners to market before everything fell apart.

"We'd like you and Eric to work together in the same positions you had before." Eric had been the company's CEO. But without the engineer to carry it off, they were left with nothing. "You'd have carte blanche in setting up the office, and in staffing." When he named a salary far above what Monroe made in his own company, he was stunned.

Monroe told the man he'd get back to him in a few days and hung up the phone. He'd gotten a few nibbles from his headhunter, but nothing as impressive as this, and not nearly the control. Often with cutbacks, you were working with a fraction of the staff needed to do the job right. Then you had to contend with inferior materials, trying to save a couple dollars on the bottom line, often finishing with an inferior product. They also had to cater to the stockholder, not necessarily make moves that were best for the company.

The one thing Monroe could say about his company was that their products were top of the line. They owned it. They didn't have to answer to stockholders who were looking for sizable profits each quarter. Which was why so many companies wanted to buy them out.

Monroe headed to the shower. If he took the job, he'd have to leave Melanie, he thought as he stepped into the spray. The warm water cascaded over his head and body, but it did nothing to ease the dread.

And every time he thought of Melanie going on without him, his need to be with her increased. He washed quickly and, after rinsing, he twisted the knob to turn off the water. Stepping out of the shower, he toweled dry.

Was she already in bed? Instead of going to bed

himself, he pulled on briefs and jeans and the first T-shirt he could find, and found himself in his car headed toward Melanie's.

Before he got there, he had second thoughts. He stopped his car in the middle of the deserted road. Except for the path his high beams lit, everything was pitch-black around him.

He couldn't lay his problems on Melanie. She had her own to contend with. All the tenants at Village Square ran to her at the slightest whiff of trouble. Half the town laid their burdens on her and she didn't need one more person knocking on her door.

He turned his car around and found himself headed to the only smoky bar in town.

The blasting music drove him inside. He wasn't much for hanging out at bars, but who could think with all the noise? He didn't want to think. He wanted to get lost in something. At least he didn't recognize anyone there. He ordered a scotch and water. The bartender set it in front of him on a non-descript white cocktail napkin but Monroe didn't drink immediately.

He was just beginning to move on in his life. Everything had happened so fast. One minute he'd owned a company. The next he'd lost it and his wife. After they'd sold, he'd stayed on at

Emerson to finish the project he'd been working on, according to the terms of their agreement. Before he'd finished, his grandmother had had the stroke.

Everything had happened at once. He hadn't settled down long enough to think, much less plot out a future. Then Melanie, like a tempest, had blown into his life. He wanted more time to get to know her. He didn't want the whirlwind courtship he'd had with Dorian. He wanted to take his time with her.

Suddenly he wanted to live again. He was ready to go on with his life. Melanie had a lot to do with that.

Monroe hadn't touched his drink. He wasn't feeling the bar scene. He walked out to the warm night breeze. Once again, he pointed his car toward Melanie's house. He didn't have to talk about his offer. He just wanted to be with her.

There were advantages to living in the middle of nowhere with no nosy neighbors to spy on you. A cover of trees blocked the view of Melanie's house from the road.

When Monroe arrived at her driveway, one lone light shone like a beacon at the end of the lane. He had second thoughts again about approaching her, but his body won out over his brain.

If he had just a short time left in Summer Lake, he wanted to spend as much of it as he could with her.

Chapter 9

Melanie had just stepped out of the shower and smoothed lotion over her skin when the doorbell rang.

Who on earth could be at her door at this time of night? Pulling on a housecoat, she went to answer it. When she peeped through the curtain she saw Monroe staring back at her.

She dragged in a deep breath and opened the door.

"Where's Courtney?" he asked.

"In bed."

With effort he moved away from her. Shoving

his hands in his pockets, he went to the family room. "What a long day."

"Is your grandmother sleeping well?"

"Like a rock." He walked over to the window and looked out into nothing.

"You seem troubled. Is she giving you a hard time?"

Monroe shook his head. He might as well say it. "I got a job offer tonight."

"Tonight?"

"The company that bought out my company offered me a new job in their new plant as chief of the technical branch." He looked at her to gauge her reaction.

"How…how soon will you be leaving?"

"I haven't accepted yet. A lot of details to work out."

"But you want it."

"It gives me more control than any other offer."

"I see. Mrs. Eudora will be disappointed to see you leave, but she'll be happy you found work you enjoy."

"What about you, Melanie?"

"If it's what you want…"

Monroe really wanted to know what she felt on a personal level.

"Courtney and I will miss you."

"I've decided to build the rink..."

"No."

"Even if I leave, I'm not selling the farm."

"No."

Monroe growled in frustration. "Why do you always fight me? When I leave here, I want to know you and Courtney will be okay."

Her chin rose. "We'll be okay."

He wasn't so sure of that. Who was he fooling? This was the woman who'd left her controlling husband and had talked a lonely old lady into building a shopping plaza. This was the woman who gave that same old lady a reason for hanging on. This was the woman who stood at a gas station in a nowhere town and saw possibilities.

She reminded him of himself so many years ago. A dreamer. She was running for mayor and there was no question that she would win. He wanted her. He needed her. He replayed his last conversation with his grandmother in his mind. But he couldn't be selfish and ask Melanie to leave these people who needed her so much.

Monroe had never felt this incredible connection with another woman—with another person, period. He didn't want to leave without Melanie.

But he couldn't farm for the rest of his life. The place ran just fine without him. He needed to work in his chosen profession and he couldn't do that here.

Melanie's smile was encouraging and accepting. She patted the seat beside her. "Come sit down and tell me about this new job."

He hadn't meant to do that. He hadn't meant to lay his burdens on her. But without hesitation, he sank to the couch beside her, needing to touch, to be near her—and began to tell her about the project he'd suggested before they'd sold. He began to relax while he discussed it. She was a great listener. And he was comfortable talking to her in a way he was never comfortable talking to Dorian. He and Dorian didn't talk about his work. They didn't talk about much of anything at all.

Was this camaraderie what his grandparents had shared? It wasn't flamboyant, or outlandish. He was...comfortable. How bland. But he felt warm inside, soothed.

How could he...how could he for a moment leave his sweet southern comfort?

The next morning as Melanie made oatmeal and cut up fruit for Courtney's breakfast, she was in one bad mood. As soon as something good came into her life, it was being snatched away.

"Courtney, you're going to be late. Come on."

Courtney ran down the stairs, tossing her backpack at the door. "I've got plenty of time. Aren't you going to eat with me?"

They usually ate their meals together. Melanie wouldn't let her melancholy carry over to Courtney. She sank into a chair and stuffed food into her mouth, but it tasted like sawdust. She pushed the plate aside.

"Do you need me to drill you on your math test?"

"I know it. Math is my favorite subject."

"Okay. Good luck."

Finished with her food, Courtney hopped up and ran to the bathroom. Coming back, she picked up her backpack.

Melanie went to the door and kissed her. She stood at the window and watched Courtney until the bus arrived, then she stacked dishes in the dishwasher and wiped down the countertop.

She was on her way to her room to dress when the doorbell rang. Frowning, she glanced through the window. Monroe's truck was in the driveway. She opened the door.

And they were in each other's arms.

"Umm, you smell good enough to eat," he said, shutting the door behind him with his foot. He didn't know what compelled him to seek out Melanie or why he'd had this sudden urgency to be with her.

"I can't wait another moment to have you. I hope you feel the same way about me."

"Yes, yes. You're so...unexpected."

"Like you're not?" He sounded almost angry as he pressed his mouth to hers again. Turning with her in his arms, he pinned her against the door. She felt the length of his body against hers and every bit of his strength. His tight torso and long, strong thighs were pressed against hers. The bulge in his pants was a definite sign he wanted her every bit as much as she wanted him.

He yanked her robe open and stood back to gaze at her.

"You always answer the door like this?" She didn't wear a stitch of clothing beneath the robe.

"I only had time to shower."

"So you wrapped up this little package just for me?"

"Yes."

"Let me show you how much I appreciate this gift."

"I can't wait."

He ducked low and took her nipple in his mouth. The pleasing sensation tore a moan from Melanie's throat. He wrapped his arms around her beneath the robe.

Melanie tugged his T-shirt over his head and tossed it to the floor. Then she felt skin hot enough to singe against her curves. And the sensations were so exquisite, another moan escaped from her.

"It's been a long time."

"Not that long."

"Feels like forever."

He tugged the robe off her shoulders, letting it pool at her feet.

She unbuttoned, unzipped his slacks.

He swung her into his arms and headed to the hallway. "Which way?"

"Straight back."

When he stopped beside the bed, he stood her on her feet. She smoothed his pants and briefs over his hips. They dropped to the floor and he stepped out of them—and stood before her as naked as her, the evidence of his desire apparent. She stroked his magnificent length.

"We have to find a way to be together," he moaned between gritted teeth.

"Let's not talk about that."

"I mean it," he said, burying his fingers in her thick hair. "I don't want to lose you."

"If you keep talking, we're going to lose the moment." She was getting depressed again.

"We can't have that, can we?" His hand feathered over her shoulders and dipped to her back.

Sinking into his cushioning embrace, she brushed tender kisses on his chest. With his hands on her hips, he dipped low to suckle on her brown nipples, bringing them to a pebbled peak. As she trailed a hand down his taut stomach to his hips, his muscles rippled under her touch.

His mouth found hers and his kiss was wild and hot. She moved her hips against his, bringing as much pleasure to herself as to him.

He swept her off her feet and placed her on the bed. Before she could grab a breath, he was kissing her calf, her thighs, tearing a moan from deep within.

Tugging on a condom, he nudged her legs apart and settled between them. Slowly, he entered her, his gaze locked with hers, and they were joined as one. Her legs wrapped around his hips, sinking him deeper inside. She kissed him long and fierce. She had waited a lifetime for this moment, her perfect match. She'd promised herself she'd never uproot her life again for a man, not ever. But at that moment, if Monroe asked her she'd leave with him, she'd shuck it all and follow him anywhere.

With her heart bursting with love and anguish, she whispered, "I…" and bit off the rest to finish with a deep moan.

Monroe's gaze jerked to hers, his breathing labored.

She couldn't let one weak moment hold him back. But her eyes must have told her story because his arms tightened around her until they were one. Closing his eyes, he buried his face into her neck and she turned her face enough to kiss his cheek. He sank deeper into her and she gasped in sweet agony.

Mounting waves of ecstasy throbbed through her until her body shook with uncontrollable spasms of pleasure. She cried out in release—and heard his harsh response before their world fell silent and still.

For long moments his weight settled on her. Then he slid to the side and gathered her into his arms. Unexpressed emotions roared between them.

A week had passed and their last coupling still left Melanie feeling out of control. She hated that.

Spring break was over and, except for locals and seniors traveling to their homes in the north for the summer, business slowed.

It was Friday and Jewel was going to pick Courtney up after school to take her to the farm to ride Rainshadow. As much as Melanie wanted to distance herself from Monroe's magnetic power, she couldn't punish Courtney. The child had aced the math test and a visit to the farm was her reward.

"I'm going to leave in five minutes if it's okay with you," Melanie's assistant Carla said.

"It's slow. I'll close up. Go on home." Melanie had started to dust when the phone rang. It was Jewel.

"Did Courtney come to the store?" she asked.

"No."

"She didn't get off the bus here. I waited near the road for her."

"Let me call home and then try Mrs. Eudora. She was angry with me this morning because I wouldn't let her wear some too-tight jeans to school."

"Call me back and let me know."

Melanie called her house. Although she didn't let Courtney go home alone, the girl had a key. Courtney didn't answer. Then Melanie called Mrs. Eudora. Courtney wasn't there, either. Melanie called a couple of her friends but she wasn't with them.

Fear sent a chill up Melanie's back.

"Can you close up so I can look for Courtney?" she asked Carla.

"You go ahead. I'll call around."

Grabbing her purse, Melanie dashed to her car and drove home as if she were in a NASCAR race. When she flew through the door she saw Courtney's backpack on the kitchen table. She called out, but Courtney didn't respond. My God. Somebody could have kidnapped her child. Fear exploded through Melanie as she ran through the house checking every room.

Courtney's school clothes where thrown on the bed and her drawers were pulled open as if she'd hurriedly searched for something else to wear, the way she usually did when she was in a hurry to get someplace. She was always in a hurry.

But had she gone out with someone? Melanie ran outside. Cupping her hands to her mouth, she called Courtney's name. She called in every direction. She heard a car tearing up her drive and went to investigate. It was Monroe.

"I was just going to check the woods around the house," Melanie told him as he alighted with the car still rocking. "She came home but I don't know where she went."

"Let's split up."

Monroe went one direction and Melanie went in the opposite direction. She'd searched for what seemed forever when she saw Monroe trooping through the woods with Courtney and Connie. He was carrying their boom box.

"Where have you been?" Melanie yelled. She wanted to shake the daylights out of both girls. Her knees were so weak, she sat on a stump to keep from sinking in a puddle in the dirt.

"I was helping Connie with her math."

"Didn't we agree you would get off the bus at Monroe's farm and your cousin would pick you up there?"

"Oh, I forgot."

"You forgot!" Melanie counted to ten to keep from strangling her child. She was still weak-kneed with terrifying thoughts of kidnapping and a million other travesties.

"Don't be mad at us. She was helping me with my homework, Mrs. Lambert. I don't understand my teacher and I failed my math test. I have to do better."

"I'm not angry that she helped you. Only that she didn't tell me where she was going and I was frightened that something bad had happened."

"You two go to the house and continue studying," Monroe said.

"Do your parents know you're here?" Melanie asked Connie.

The child shook her head.

"Call them as soon as you get to the house and let them know where you are."

"But you're Carsons. I can't be caught with you."

"Call your parents," Monroe demanded.

The child jerked back. "Can I tell them you're helping me with soccer?"

"Your parents aren't going to mind that you're getting help with your homework," Melanie said.

"You don't understand…"

Melanie waved her away. "Go ahead. Just as long as they know where you are."

The girls rushed off and Melanie sat stiffly. Adrenaline born of fear still raced through her body. Unable to stop shaking like a leaf, she clasped her hands together and her temper flared.

"There's something definitely wrong when a child has to say she's playing soccer instead of working on her homework. I'm so fed up with this feud I could wring some necks. How can adults do this to children?"

"Come here."

In D.C., Melanie had been away from her family. Their support came from a thousand miles away. She couldn't go calling them every time she ran into trouble. And her husband was no support at all. She learned early on to depend on herself. She'd stood alone so long that it felt foreign to share her anguish. At first she stiffened in Monroe's arms, then she slowly relaxed against his strong shoulders. Moments passed before she realized his arms were around her.

She couldn't afford the luxury of relying on him. He was leaving her. With a deep sigh, she sank into his embrace. Who's to say she couldn't enjoy his comfort? He was here now and she felt the reassuring beating of his heart against her.

"I have to go," she said.

"I'll call Connie's mother and take the girls with me." Rising, he wrapped his arm around her shoulder and together they walked back to the house.

Melanie's purse was in the car, her keys in her hand. She drove directly to Uncle Milton's farm.

Uncle Milton and Elmore were squaring off again, Uncle Milton pointing a hoe at Elmore and Elmore pointing a shovel at Uncle Milton while they shouted at each other from opposite sides of the road.

Aunt Thelma picked her salad greens as if the

two men weren't trying to kill each other right in front of her.

Melanie hopped out of her car and hurried toward them. "Just stop it you two. This feud has got to stop!"

"It'll stop when the last Hicks is off of Carson land."

"This Hicks is never going to leave."

Like rams, they charged each other to the middle of the road, jabbing and ducking.

"Just stop it before someone gets hurt," Melanie shouted. "You've got families. How can you do this? You're crazy old fools." Her words had no effect.

A car slammed on its brakes. The men broke apart, waited for the car to pass and got right back at it.

"You're going to get killed." Melanie ran to them, tried to tug them apart.

"Get back here, Melanie." For the first time, Aunt Thelma intervened, but the men ignored her, until finally Melanie got between them, thinking she was the craziest fool of all.

"Get out of there, Melanie." She caught a glimpse of Aunt Thelma running toward her.

"Each of you go on your own land."

They glared at each other while they backed up to the shoulders of the road. Melanie leaned against her car.

Aunt Thelma looked at her husband. "You think you can get back to hoeing the crabgrass before it overtakes my vegetables?"

Winded, he gave her a disgruntled look and marched off toward his field, only to turn back to face the two women.

She ripped into Melanie. "Don't you *ever* put yourself in danger getting between those two again. If they want to kill themselves, let 'em. There's no one more stubborn than an old fool."

"What brings you out here?" Leaning on his hoe, Uncle Milton threw a disgruntled glance at his wife.

"I came to talk to you."

"What about?"

Melanie marched over to him with her hands on her hips. "This feud has to stop, Uncle Milton. It's gone on long enough."

"There're things you don't understand since you didn't grow up 'round here. Family is everything. Rebecca was my aunt. One of the kindest persons I've ever known."

He started chopping wild grass and Melanie followed him down the row. "So many people walk around all important. They have high-paying jobs. Huge houses. Drive expensive cars. But what do they have inside?" He pounded a fist against his chest. "The woman sleeping next to him? What does she think of him? What about his children? Do they know he loves them more 'em he loves himself? Do they know he'd die for 'em?"

He spread his arms wide. "I'm just a plain farmer. But my family is everything to me. I can give up the farm. I can give up the house. But my wife, my children, my grandchildren—I can't give them up. That's what I learned from my father. What he learned from his father. Because when your family's gone, there's nothing left.

"It wasn't that Mark Hicks stole the land so much as how he did it. It's that he thought so little of Rebecca, he flushed away her life before she really had a chance to live it. Took up with a woman right here in town and moved her onto Rebecca's land." He pointed a finger toward Elmore's farm. "That woman's children live off Rebecca's land. So don't tell me that her death meant nothing. A Hicks got no business living off her land when one of them took what was most precious away from her."

Melanie's heart sank. Uncle Milton was going to

let that sore fester in his heart until the day he died. And the legacy he left behind, his children, were going to carry it with them. There was no end in sight.

Defeat clogged Melanie's throat. "I only know that spreading hatred isn't healthy."

"I don't hate them."

"I want my daughter happy, Uncle Milton."

"She is happy. She's got a whole bunch of family round her who loves her. She's like a ball of sunshine running round. You can't protect her from everything."

He was so stubborn in being right, he didn't see the harm the feud caused.

"But the girls play so well together on the soccer team."

"They're playing a game. You can't do nothing about this feud, girl. You didn't start it. You can't end it."

In that moment Melanie wanted to tuck Courtney under her heart and move as far away from this rancor as she could get.

With his calloused hand, her uncle patted hers. "Go on now and let this old man get to work." His gaze was so tender, love just poured out of him and wrapped her in, cuddling her up like a blanket. How could she make him see that the feud was taking away from that? How could he not find room in his life beyond family?

Courtney had love here. Among her cousins, uncles and aunts, she'd found love she'd never find in another setting. But that love came with an enormous price.

Melanie started back to her car. Aunt Thelma hugged her. She understood what Melanie was suffering, but she'd given up on a solution a long time ago.

Melanie doesn't need him, Monroe thought. What could he offer the woman who already had everything that counted?

Before he started his day's chores, he visited his grandmother. She was eating breakfast on the morning porch and catching a warm breeze. The morning sun glowed on huge pots of flowers. Dressed in slacks and a short-sleeved top, his grandmother was livelier from her daily walks through her blooming garden.

"Join us for breakfast," she said.

Mrs. Pearl stood. "There's plenty. I can cook you an egg if you want it."

"I've already had breakfast, thank you." A china teapot was placed next to a coffeepot. Mrs.

Pearl wasn't a tea drinker the way his grandmother was. Monroe got himself a cup and poured coffee into it.

"Well, I'll get these dishes done while you all have a nice visit."

Monroe sat in the chair Mrs. Pearl had vacated.

"I talked to Melanie the other day and mentioned that Courtney was welcome to get off the bus at my house and stay here until she got off work, but she wanted to wait a few weeks. Can't you talk to her Monroe? I miss having Courtney around. And I can help her with homework."

"She probably thinks you need time for your therapy and other things."

"I know what I'm capable of doing. I miss the girl. And have you done anything about that riding rink?"

"Melanie said Courtney was too busy to ride."

"She'd stop the excuses if you married her."

"Woman, you're out of your mind."

"Just forget I said anything."

"Don't even try using your psychology on me." He stood. "Do you need anything?"

"Not a thing."

"I'll be back at nine tomorrow for your doctor's appointment."

"I'll be ready, although Pearl can take me."

"I've got it covered."

When Monroe made it home, he was still reeling from his grandmother's statement. *Marry Melanie.* As if he'd do that again. As if she'd have him.

He almost missed Eric sitting in a lawn chair in the front yard. Monroe stopped in the middle of a step. Pain, shock, joy, fury—all kinds of emotions slammed into each other.

A lifetime ago, the two had been best friends.

This was the first time the two had confronted each other since the company breakup.

"Hello, Monroe."

At the sound of Eric's voice, Monroe blocked his feelings and continued up the walk. "Come in," Monroe said. It was time to get that first awkward meeting over with.

Monroe tossed his hat on the coat tree. "Can I get you anything?" What did you say to a friend turned enemy?

"Nothing. I guess you got the call from Emerson."

"I did, but I'm going to decline." The men squared off against each other.

"You got a better offer?"

"The four of us working together again? I don't think so. When the going gets tough, you'll bail."

"It was more than that…."

"Right."

"Laying it all on me is convenient, isn't it? And I let you in the beginning, because…"

"Because what?"

"Look. You were going after Aaron with a vengeance. It was tough to get business done. Hell, half the time we were breaking up fights."

"I did my job."

"You broke Aaron's nose for chrissake, loosened two of his teeth. And you were on his back about everything."

"He wasn't doing his job. You should have replaced him instead of disbanding the entire company."

Eric sighed. "I know the company was your baby. But it wasn't going to survive Aaron's faithlessness. It couldn't survive your divorce."

"It's over and done with. I'm not signing up with another deal with you all again."

"The offer wasn't made to all of us. Only you and me. You know, siding with them was the worst thing I ever did. If I'd believed for a moment the company could survive, I wouldn't have." Walking to the fireplace, Eric raked a hand over his head. "We started getting more and more offers for buyouts and Peter had wanted to sell and take the profits." Eric sighed. "I guess we didn't do a great job of choosing partners."

"Guess not."

"I want this, Monroe. But I can't do it without you. This time we'll have more discretional funds. We'll have time for a life. I don't want the job to be my life ever again."

"You think it'll be different with Emerson? Stockholders want profits, and you don't get that without working long hours."

"I've already discussed that with Emerson. I told them if they want that kind of manager, hire someone else."

"Good luck."

Eric looked disappointed. "I'm going to drop by Mrs. Eudora's. She said she was feeling better."

"She is."

"You've got a nice farm here, Monroe."

"How...how is Eric Jr.?"

"Having a great soccer season. School's great."

Monroe didn't know what made him say "Bring him out here sometime. He'd love the animals."

For the first time since he'd arrived, Eric smiled. "I'll do that."

"Tell Veronica hello for me."

"She's at the hotel. She'd love to see you."

He could imagine Veronica's impression of their rinky-dink hotel. "How long will you be in town?"

"Through the weekend. Thought we'd visit Savannah while we're here."

"And Eric Jr.?"

"Veronica's parents are keeping him while we're away."

As much as Monroe didn't want Eric under his roof, Veronica was still a good friend. He couldn't let her remain in that dingy motel. "Why don't you stay at the house? It's big enough." For him to get lost in. He wouldn't have to see Eric.

"Veronica would love that. She's done nothing but complain about the hotel." He rose, jiggled his keys. "Good to see you again, Monroe."

When Eric left, Monroe called Mrs. Pearl to see if a staff member could work every day to ensure that Ronnie could take a mini vacation. He knew her. She had to keep busy. She'd be looking for things to do. The only thing he wanted her to do was take walks along the lake, enjoy his pool and ride his animals. He didn't want her to worry about cooking breakfast or making her bed. She needed a break.

Of course Mrs. Pearl wanted to know why he needed someone to work every day, nosy woman.

Chapter 10

The next day, Melanie was still reeling from her ordeal with Uncle Milton when Monroe showed up at her shop.

"You and Courtney settle things?" he asked.

"She still won't admit to people that she's teaching Connie math, and Connie is afraid to admit her connection to Courtney. Darn it. The girls are building a friendship they can't acknowledge. It's such a mess."

"Feuds often are. You're dealing with stubborn people."

"What an understatement. I just want to bang their heads together. Knock some sense into them." After venting, some of the anger drained out of Melanie, replaced by despair. "Uncle Milton is never going to forgive. Both men think they're right. Neither is willing to relent even a little."

"Melanie, you take on the world. Don't anguish over this. Sometimes things have a way of working out on their own."

"You don't really believe that, do you?"

Monroe nodded. "Yes, I do."

"Thanks for trying to cheer me up. I'm just in a rotten mood."

"Guess I came at a bad time, hmm?"

She really looked at him for the first time. He seemed troubled and here she was pouring out her problems on him. He'd been a rock for her yesterday. "Thanks for being there for me. It's not a bad time. I just need something to take my mind off the feud."

His eyes were gentle and uncertain. "Look, an old partner of mine is in town with his wife. I was hoping I could convince you to join us for dinner tomorrow night. My grandmother would love to have Courtney stay with her overnight, if you're worried about her being up too late."

"I think I can be persuaded," she said with a teasing smile that drew his focus. "It'll be six before I can get there. Is that okay?"

"Six works for me. Mind if Courtney gets off the bus at Grandma's?"

"I'll tell her tonight. If she can get within a foot of Mrs. Eudora it shouldn't be a problem. I guess you'll probably be busy with your guests today."

"Eric and Veronica are moving into my house as we speak. But stop by so I can introduce you."

"I can't; I have a meeting later on, but I'll be there tomorrow."

Monroe gathered her into his arms. "This is going to be a stressful week. Thanks for agreeing to come."

"Eric. Was he your friend?" Melanie frowned. She could tell Monroe disliked talking about his past.

His gray eyes became flat and unreadable. "We were best friends."

"Sounds like you might want him to be a best friend again. Maybe now that time has passed you can talk things through."

"You're still the dreamer, aren't you?"

Maybe that was how Uncle Milton saw her, too. People saw her as the dreamer. Not to be taken seriously. Maybe that was why Monroe could swat away her concerns about the feud like a pesky mosquito.

Monroe's family was scattered over the globe. If he couldn't talk to his best friend, then more than likely he hadn't confided in anyone. "Why are they here?"

"Remember the job offer I had from Emerson? They want to hire Eric as CEO of the subsidiary they're forming."

"Just like old times. How do you feel about working with him again?"

"I don't know if we can."

But he moved the man and his wife into his home and he wanted her to meet them. Even though they were still on the outs, these people were obviously important to Monroe.

"Well, first of all, how do you feel about working for Emerson?"

For the first time, she saw a spark of interest in his eyes. "They want me to spearhead a project I recommended before we sold. It's a project I'd like to do."

"Can you be content with Emerson? Can you go from a business owner to an employee?"

"I don't know. I thought I could. But owning your own company, especially something that's cutting-edge, is a lot of work. Takes enormous capital. We couldn't afford the staff Emerson is offering us."

She gave him a little rub on his arm. "You'll work it out."

"Yeah—there goes that dreamer again."

Melanie struggled to smile so he wouldn't see how much his words hurt. "What kind of books does Veronica like?"

"Fiction, I guess. How would I know?"

She scoffed. "That helps a lot. Do you know how many categories there are under fiction?"

He touched his fingertips to one side of her jaw. With a shrug, he was out the door, the weight of his future riding on his shoulders. Melanie watched him as he climbed into his truck and drove off.

She started back around the countertop. The telephone rang.

"Melanie," Mrs. Eudora announced in a commanding voice. "Please drop by this evening if it's convenient. I have some plaza business to discuss with you."

Melanie had planned to work on the business plan with Gail after work, but she couldn't afford to alienate Mrs. Eudora. "What time?" she asked.

"After you leave the shop. Courtney is here with your cousin. Since you're coming by anyway she may as well stay until you get here. I'll make sure she completes all her homework."

"Thank you, Mrs. Eudora."

"Pearl has already prepared dinner, dear. I'll let Courtney eat so she won't go to bed on a full stomach if it's okay with you."

"That's fine." *Good excuse to visit with my daughter,* Melanie thought.

"She's in good hands. Don't worry about her."

"I never worry when she's with you."

Melanie hung up. By hook or crook, Mrs. Eudora was getting Courtney over there. At least Melanie wouldn't have to worry about the child hiding in the woods. Mrs. Eudora kept an eagle eye on her. And Courtney admired the older woman.

Melanie called Gail and asked if they could meet later. Gail complied.

Melanie glanced up as the door opened and the little bell above tinkled. The mayor strutted in, his chest puffed out, followed by a man dressed in a polo shirt and khaki slacks.

A woman on the city council followed them in. "Afternoon, Melanie. Oh, Andrew. I wanted to have a word with you," the woman said.

"Just a moment," the mayor replied, and went to a secluded corner with the woman.

The man who was with him stood at the far

reaches of the store when Andrew came tearing to the counter.

"I don't know what you think you're up to, but you can forget becoming mayor of this town. I've been mayor for fifteen years and no outsider is coming in to take my place."

"Maybe the people feel it's time for new blood," Melanie said calmly, glad to get one up on him for a change. She was sick of him threatening their jobs.

"The way things are run is just fine. We don't need you."

"Maybe the citizens of this town feel they can do better than a mayor who has done nothing to bring jobs here, but is sure bent on trying to take them away."

"If these companies expand the shops, they'll bring in even more jobs, and you know it. You're trying your best to ruin me, but that isn't going to happen."

"I'm not trying to ruin you. I'm trying to survive. To carve out a living for my family, just like the other shop owners. Why is it so important for you to stop us?"

"Because we don't need an outsider coming in telling the little folks what to do. You'll never be mayor of Summer Lake."

"May the best person win the office."

The woman on the city council came to the cash register with two books. "I've been looking forward to reading these for ages. It's nice to have a local bookstore. And you keep a great selection here, Melanie."

"Thank you. Did you find everything you were looking for?"

"Oh, yes."

As Melanie rang up the sale, she noticed the mayor and the man leaving her store and crossing the street. Melanie smiled. He had lost his strut.

Melanie was only at Mrs. Eudora's for a short time. Mrs. Pearl had left out a plate for Melanie. Baked lemon chicken, broccoli with new red potatoes, finishing with a tall glass of lemonade and warm yeast rolls.

Melanie had worked alone most of the day and was glad to let her tired feet rest. Courtney and Mrs. Pearl played checkers while Melanie and Mrs. Eudora talked

"I understand Monroe's ex was at one of the games with her new baby. How did he react?"

"He seemed okay. He didn't actually see the baby up close."

"Heard she came over to speak to him."

"A brief conversation. Did Monroe say anything about it?"

"Oh, pooh. He's so close-mouthed. Take my head off if I say one word."

Melanie didn't know how much to divulge, but the woman worried about Monroe.

"He didn't seem bothered by her. That's all I know."

"The poor dear loves children. It's a good thing Courtney likes him. She's a godsend for both of us." Mrs. Eudora reached across the table and patted Melanie's hand. "And you're just an angel sent from heaven for poor Monroe. He's taken with you."

"You're just a crafty old woman, you know that?"

Mrs. Eudora squeezed her lips and lifted her chin. "It's the truth."

The woman was determined to have her way.

"Melanie, I don't see why Courtney can't get off the bus here sometimes like she used to."

"I wasn't trying to keep her from you. You have therapy. You don't need the extra stress."

"If I get tired, Pearl's here. I'm never here alone. Courtney's good company. And I'm teaching her how to knit scarves. How will she ever learn if she doesn't come here? She has to learn those skills."

"Between Aunt Thelma teaching her how to can preserves and you knitting, she's learning lots of new skills." Melanie sighed. "I guess we can work something out if it isn't too much for you." Monroe was going to have a fit, but that was his problem. If he didn't like it, he could take it up with Eudora.

It was another half hour before Melanie left with Courtney. Gail was waiting for her when she arrived home. The women spent three hours updating descriptions of the business, marketing information and financial data.

"Good thing we prepared all this before you presented the plan to Mrs. Eudora," Gail said.

"Gosh, we spent months on that. See if you can get sales figures from the stores for the weeks of spring break."

"You collect them from the Hickses, and I'll get them from everyone else."

"The feud can't interfere with business."

Gail blew out a long breath and they finished as much as they could.

The next day, Melanie left work early to dress for dinner. She must have spent an hour in her closet trying things on and discarding them. Whatever Monroe said, Eric and his wife were still important to him. She wondered what kind of people they were if Eric hadn't stood up for his friend.

She settled on beige slacks, a red V-neck top and red strappy sandals. She complemented the outfit with gold accessories.

She could have driven, but Monroe insisted on coming to get her. He asked her to bring sneakers in case they went for a walk. Although he tried to hide it, he was apprehensive.

At his house, a beautiful woman with short black hair and ebony tones stood in the yard admiring roses. A man, approximately six feet tall, stood beside her with his hands deep in his pockets.

"Melanie, meet Veronica and Eric Parker."

Melanie extended a hand. "Pleased to meet you."

Veronica clasped a warm hand around hers. "It's our pleasure. I hope you're hungry, because the aromas coming out of that kitchen are heavenly."

"I'm starved."

When she scanned Eric's troubled gaze, she realized there was a hidden story Monroe hadn't touched on. And although Veronica was outgoing and Monroe was clearly indulgent with her, she, too, hid a world of concern about him.

Eric may have betrayed Monroe, but it was apparent these people were concerned.

"I have a gift for you." Melanie handed the bag of goodies to Veronica. "Welcome to Summer Lake."

"You shouldn't have, but thank you." Setting the bag on a table, she pulled out the book. Her eyes softened. "I love this author, but I hadn't gotten her latest yet. How wonderful." Then she took out the box with the figurine.

"The gifts, both of them, are perfect. Eric rushed me out so quickly I didn't have time to pack any books. And the delicate bird figurine, it's gorgeous." She hugged Melanie. "This is so thoughtful, isn't it, Eric? I have just the place for it in my living room."

"Very thoughtful, thank you, Melanie. So, when do we eat?" he asked.

Veronica tapped him on the arm. "You're always thinking with your stomach."

The table was set up on the screened back porch. A crisp white tablecloth was topped with candles and small vases of fresh lavender and purple lisianthus. White china and purple napkins complemented the arrangement.

A warm breeze blew off the lake, but not enough to keep the mosquitoes away. The two couples rushed to the porch, the screen door snapping shut behind them.

"Would you like a glass of wine?" Monroe asked.

Melanie nodded while trying to size up his guests. They tried to act as if nothing was wrong.

Melanie ate more than anyone else. She felt like a pig because the others only picked at their food. The performance was a drain on all of them, Monroe included. After dinner, the men went to saddle the horses while the ladies cleaned up.

"I'm going to change shoes, then we can meet the men on the lake," Melanie said.

"Sounds good to me."

By the time Melanie changed into sneakers, Veronica was waiting for her. They strolled to the beach. The orange ball of sun was just beginning to lower over the water, casting a picturesque glimmer on the water.

"Are you serious about Monroe?" Veronica asked abruptly. "Because I won't have him hurt again."

"I'm not the one who hurt him," Melanie retorted.

The fight seemed to drain from Veronica like a deflating balloon. "Eric and I both love Monroe like a brother, probably more. It…" Her voice caught. "Having to vote against Monroe ripped Eric apart. He couldn't sleep for months. Monroe…Monroe locked him out—completely.

Wouldn't have anything to do with him. I'm surprised he didn't lock me out, as well. I don't know why he kept that door open, but it's given us hope over the last two years that maybe Eric and he could find a way to patch things up."

Veronica gazed at the lake as if it held the answers to her dilemma. "I've sent Christmas cards, birthday cards. He never responds. And when I call, the conversations are stilted. It's a wonder Mrs. Eudora continued to talk to us."

Melanie cleared her clogged throat. "He invited you into his home. There's hope there."

"Do you love him?" Veronica asked.

"It's not easy to answer that question."

"Sure it is. Either you love him or you don't," the woman said sharply.

"Love is the easy part. Making it work is what's hard. Monroe doesn't love me."

"Don't be silly. I know him. He loves you."

"You care about him, don't you?"

"Eric and I both care about him. Dorian…You know it wasn't the fact that she left him that was so horrible. She could have gone about it another way. She had an affair with his friend. That isn't easy to overcome."

"I know," Melanie said. "It was like the domino

effect. Her affair destroyed not only her marriage, but four friendships, and a business."

"They worked so hard to put that company together. I don't miss it though. Don't get me wrong. I thought it was good, but I never saw Eric. We had begun to fight because I felt I was in the marriage alone."

"You survived it and you both look to be stronger for it."

Veronica glanced down the shore to where the men walked toward them with the horses. Her eyes warmed at the sight of her husband.

Melanie envied the couple's companionship. They weren't just two people who shared the same address and a piece of paper. They were truly an extension of each other. Whatever the world threw them, it was obvious they weathered the storm together. It was the key ingredient that had been missing in her marriage to Bruce.

Oh, Melanie had tried. She stayed up nights hoping for intimate conversations. But Bruce was always too tired to talk. She'd tried to carve out time for them, but he never returned the effort. Finally, she stopped trying. She'd learned early on that one person couldn't hold a marriage together.

Couples like Veronica and Eric always came

out on top because the outside world wasn't their barometer. The people inside their home counted the most.

"What're you all talking about up there?" Eric asked.

"You," his wife said playfully.

Monroe and Eric caught up with them and Melanie took the reins of her horse.

"Need help?" Monroe asked as she mounted.

"Who do you think usually rides with Courtney?"

"Then why don't you ever come with her to ride?" He patted the horse's head.

"I didn't want a run-in with the Beast."

"Chicken."

She leaned over and stuck out her tongue at him. He caught her by the shoulders and kissed her. The surge of physical awareness took her by surprise, melting her all the way to her toes. She touched his chest, felt his body heat, smelled his cologne. Her stomach lurched with unmistakable desire. For an instant they forgot they weren't alone.

Monroe lifted his head and laughed, the sound rich and free, and mounted his horse in one graceful movement. The others had discreetly put distance between them.

He looked down at her, a faint light twinkling in the depths of his eyes.

Melanie was happy. It was a fleeting thing, she knew. Life had taught her that. She wished she could grasp the moment and hold on to it for a lifetime.

Melanie sat prettily on her horse. Monroe felt lighthearted and free. She had the knack of making him forget. The tides washed against the shore as they urged the horses into a light canter.

"What a gorgeous sunset," she said.

"Spectacular." She rode slightly ahead of him and he was commenting on her backside, not the sunset.

They rode three miles out until they got to a rock where she and Monroe had spent an afternoon. They alighted from the horses and tethered them to a young tree nearby. Eric and Veronica were already waiting for them.

"How did you and Eric meet?" Melanie asked Monroe.

"We were roommates our freshman year of college and we remained roommates throughout except for the year I attended MIT on an exchange program."

"I didn't know you attended MIT."

He nodded.

"After he left Morehouse, he returned there to get his doctorate," Veronica said.

These details made Melanie realize how much she didn't know about Monroe.

"He's so low-key about everything," Veronica continued. "You'd never know he's one of the country's top scientific minds. Which is why so many companies want him."

He had to take the offer from Emerson. Melanie definitely couldn't keep him in Summer Lake. It wouldn't be fair. She reached for his hand. He was here now, and she needed the contact.

He kissed the back of her hand before setting his arm around her shoulder, drawing her close. She leaned her head on his chest and inhaled the heady mixture of man, cologne. She snuggled closer. Evenings with Monroe were limited and she planned to enjoy every moment left.

Sitting on the rock, they looked west where the sun had all but disappeared into the horizon. When it set completely, Monroe cupped her chin and tilted it. He lowered his mouth to hers and kissed her.

"It's very beautiful here," Veronica said. "I imagine it doesn't get very cold."

"We have a few cold days. But most of the time it doesn't go below fifty."

"That sounds heavenly to me. I hate cold winters."

"Wait until July, then you'll be crying for snow."

"I don't think so. I can get used to this. Monroe, I hope you plan to keep this place. All you need is a tennis court and every time you turn around I'll be here vacationing."

"Feel free to come anytime, Ronnie."

"Don't forget you offered, because I won't."

Veronica came to the bookstore to buy more books afterward and Melanie took her to lunch at the diner. Melanie took the rest of the day off and they boated and swam. On Friday night they double-dated in Savannah—dinner at Paula Deen's restaurant and a play.

Monroe hosted the season's soccer party on Saturday. They set up an awning in his yard with a couple of tables beneath it for food and drinks. He hired a lifeguard for the pool and someone provided a boom box that blasted music.

Grandmothers sat under shady trees fanning themselves. One of the kids played the *Beauty and the Beast* CD. Monroe asked Melanie to dance with him.

The moment he touched her, the surge of physical awareness assailed her, taking her completely by surprise. It felt as if someone had sucked half the oxygen out of the air. Her eyes lifted to his and his hand caressed her back. He was so tall and handsome in his sky-blue polo shirt and khaki slacks. They'd never danced together before, Melanie thought, and Monroe knew how to move.

She smiled.

"What's so funny," Monroe asked.

"This song reminds me of us."

"You think I was a beast? Was I that bad?"

"Afraid so. Until you changed."

"You like fairy tales."

With the music playing in the background, being held close to Monroe, she felt as if she were part of her very own fairy tale. Yes, he'd been completely horrible when they'd met at his house. But he'd revealed a completely opposite side of himself, and she liked the change.

And she'd fallen in love with him. My God. She loved him. The realization almost made her stumble.

He pulled her close, and she buried her face in his neck and inhaled his essence.

They danced as if they were the only ones in existence, and for a moment, Melanie forgot they weren't alone. Monroe's hand tangled in her hair and when she looked up, his lips touched hers.

She closed her eyes, feeling the strength of his body, his steady heartbeat against her chest.

In the back of her mind, Melanie heard the words that seemed to be made just for them. *Tale as old as time…Beauty and the Beast.*

The song ended, and Melanie opened her eyes. Monroe's arms remained around her for several seconds while they stared into each other's eyes…until she heard the kids clapping and their teasing voices.

She and Monroe moved apart awkwardly. Her eyes alighted on Mrs. Eudora's first, as the older woman wiped tears from her cheeks.

Her feelings were written all over her face.

Monroe had to figure out what he wanted in his life. Melanie wouldn't cloud his mind with her sappy feelings.

The next day after church, Melanie went to the store and hid in her office to fill out book and CD orders. A bunch of kids were always hanging out in the CD section. Even when books didn't sell, the kids bought CDs. MP3 players hadn't made it to Summer Lake yet.

She and Courtney had been invited to dinner at Mrs. Eudora's, which meant that Monroe would probably be there. She was trying to finish up her order so they could head out.

She was almost finished when Veronica walked in.

"All ready to leave?" Melanie asked.

"Almost. We're leaving for home in an hour. I haven't enjoyed any vacation more. I wanted to get some gifts and tell you those figurines make gift buying easy."

"The artist is local. We do a brisk business with tourists."

"I can understand why." She sighed. "I enjoyed the week so much. And most of all I've enjoyed my time with you. Monroe has changed so much. I think that has a lot to do with you."

"You're giving me more credit than I deserve."

"I don't think so."

"Well, you have to come back and bring your son when he's out of school."

"He'll love it. Please come with Monroe when he visits. I'll show you the city. And bring Courtney."

If she and Monroe were together that long. Melanie hugged her. "Keep in touch." It wasn't often she clicked with a virtual stranger, but Veronica and she had hit it off immediately.

"I'm working on Monroe."

Melanie laughed. "Don't bother."

"I'm serious."

"So am I." Melanie tilted her chin. "It has to come naturally. He has to know I'm the one he wants, or I don't want any part of him."

"You don't understand. I almost left Eric. I was raising our son alone, and that wasn't the life I wanted either. So I told him I was leaving. I packed my bags and moved to my parents' home. It drove Eric crazy. I think it's one of the reasons he sold out. Peter's wife had already left him. So you see, Monroe's marriage wasn't the only marriage falling apart. The company had hit it big. The hours kept getting longer and longer." She shook her head. "Eric kept saying that it would get better, but it never did. And I'd had it. I couldn't make him change. So I had to do what I thought was best for the children and me."

"I'm sorry. You seem so perfect together, now."

"I don't think Eric ever told Monroe I left him. But I didn't leave my husband for another man. I don't think I will ever meet another man I love as much as I love Eric. When I left him I knew that. Dorian was weak. Monroe doesn't understand that. You're strong. You're a fighter. He needs a strong woman."

Melanie glanced down at the desk, not seeing a

thing but the image of Monroe's face. The image of friends torn apart. Dorian, Dorian, Dorian. She was sick of the woman.

"He has to know that."

Veronica stood and so did Melanie. "Sometimes it takes a brick upside the head before they recognize it."

Melanie laughed. "You've got that right."

The women hugged.

In the week they'd been together, Melanie and Veronica had become good friends. They agreed to e-mail each other. Even though Veronica joked about vacationing in Summer Lake, it seemed unlikely they would actually see each other again.

Eric came to renew their friendship and get Monroe back to Philly where he belonged. Melanie was sure he'd accomplished both goals.

Melanie now had to face a stark reality. Her time left with Monroe was limited. She sighed. How she'd miss him.

He would be leaving soon for the world he was meant to be a part of. A world without Melanie or Summer Lake.

Chapter 11

When Monroe saw his grandmother's car coming up the lane, he charged out of the house. What was she doing driving so soon? But when the car stopped and Mrs. Pearl emerged from the driver's side and his grandmother opened the passenger door, he marched toward the car.

"I told her she should let you come to her but she wouldn't hear of it," Mrs. Pearl said.

"Just keep the motor warm," his grandmother demanded as if a bee had gotten up her skirt. "This won't take long."

Monroe took her arm to help her to the house, but she shook him off. "Why didn't you call me? You didn't have to come here."

"Because I didn't want any nosy folks listening to me when I tear into you."

"Tear into me?" It was too early in the morning for this. What was she up to now?

"Yes, you."

He opened the door and she marched straight to the kitchen.

"Who told you you could sell my business? If you ever think of selling something of mine without my permission, I'll serve you up for Sunday dinner. I didn't work all my life to have my decisions made for me. And to collude with that no-account, lazy mayor?"

Monroe held up a hand. "Just wait a minute. I didn't sell anything of yours."

"You had the mayor look for buyers for my shops."

"At the time he mentioned there were buyers interested, you were in the hospital. I didn't know if you'd want to deal with the plaza after you recovered. And he'd told a few fabrications about Melanie."

"Like what?"

He was getting irritated. "That she was taking

advantage of you. And when I saw the piddling amount your tenants paid for rent, it seemed true—until I discussed it with your lawyer."

"Well, it would do her good if she never married you after the stunt you pulled. You think I'm crazy? You think I don't have enough sense to know she's a good woman?"

Monroe shook his head. The only thing he heard was "Married?"

"If you've got the sense God gave you, you'd marry that girl."

"You don't know what you're talking about, woman."

"Humph. That's what you think. You need to be more than book smart." Crossing her arms, she glared at him as if he were a kid. But he wasn't a kid and he glared right back. "Well, I've fixed it so you and the mayor can't do a thing to hurt those people. Melanie has worked so hard for this community. She has lots of great ideas. The mayor hasn't done a thing except try to stop her, instead of listening for a change."

"I know that now," he snapped.

"I've changed the rental agreement to a buyout. I'm financing the loan for the tenants. If they own the plaza outright, then the mayor doesn't have a reason to waste his time bringing these outsiders to our town to stir up trouble. Now what do you have to say about that?" Her glare was so triumphant, Monroe had to cough to keep from laughing.

He held up both hands. "Not a thing."

"Just like that?"

"Grandma, I was only concerned that the plaza was too much for you."

"Six little units? Don't be ridiculous," she scoffed. She pulled out a kitchen chair and dropped into it. "I was floundering for a while, it's true. With your grandfather gone, I'd lost my footing. I was depressed. Your grandfather and I always worked together and we were married a long time. More than fifty years. But when Melanie came in with fresh ideas, it made me think of him. All brimming with hope." She pierced Monroe with her stare. "She's a good woman. And if you let her get away, then you're not the man I thought you were." She stood. "I'm ready to go home and take a nap."

Deep in thought, Monroe walked her to the car. "Get that nonsense about marriage out of your head."

"Is that the only thing you heard?"

"I heard plenty."

She shook her head as if he were simple. "I'm going to be Melanie's campaign manager."

"Absolutely not. It's too much for you."

"What do you know? Since when did I need a young whelp telling me what to do? You go back to Philadelphia or wherever you want to go. We'll do fine without you. Some man with good sense will come along and marry Melanie. Good woman like that don't stay single for long."

She did not need to say that. Just the thought of another man with Melanie set his back teeth on edge. Monroe sighed, the anger draining out of him. Eudora wanted him to stay. She thought marrying Melanie would keep him in town. Go figure. The best job falls in his lap and he had to debate whether he should even take it.

"*I'm* going to be her campaign manager," Monroe muttered. "We'll just get in each other's way. Just haven't gotten around to telling her yet."

Eudora's eyes lit up with a ray of hope before they dimmed, making him feel guilty. "I don't know how you're going to manage anything from Philadelphia."

"Just let me worry about it." Why was she doing this to him?

"If I were her, I wouldn't have you."

"There's no pleasing you, is there? Just go home. Do your therapy or something." She always had to be contrary. He hugged her thin shoulders and felt guilty for fighting with her. Sighing, she got in her car. As Mrs. Pearl pulled off, Monroe heard her asking what they'd discussed.

Monroe didn't want to leave Eudora alone with no family around. His father was talking about retiring soon, but knowing the older man, it would be years before he actually retired.

For the first time, Monroe realized he was in that sandwich generation he'd read so much about. More often it was women who were left with the caretaking.

The car drove out of sight. Monroe went back into the house. Eric and Ronnie wanted to take one last walk, so Monroe took the opportunity to call Melanie before she left home for work. But before he could dial the number, Anthony, his farm manager, knocked on the back door, came in and headed straight for the coffeepot. Then Melanie arrived before the man even took a sip.

"You're just in time to hear good news," Anthony said to Melanie.

"What?" she asked.

"One of our alpacas won first prize at the national championship. We've been offered eighty grand for her crias."

"Crias?" Melanie asked. "What's that?"

"A baby alpaca."

"You were offered that much for one little alpaca? Imagine that. Congratulations," Melanie said. "They're too expensive for Courtney to play with."

"She's not going to hurt them," Monroe said. He was pleased with the offer, but he wasn't a rancher and he really couldn't get worked up over the alpaca business. But thinking of baby alpacas made him wonder what Melanie had looked like pregnant.

"More than triple what we usually make," Anthony continued.

"That's wonderful," Melanie exclaimed. "You must be very pleased."

"We had five make the top four in championship shows this year. Every championship showing increases the price of the babies."

"How many female alpacas do you have?" Melanie asked.

"Fifteen dams."

"So what do they sell for when they don't make championships?" she asked.

"Twenty-two five."

"As in twenty-two thousand five hundred dollars?"

Anthony laughed. "Yeah."

"I didn't know their babies brought that much."

"It's still a rare business in this country."

"Mrs. Eudora gave me a sweater and scarf made from their fleece for Christmas last year. I was amazed at how soft it is."

"Far different from sheep's wool. That's why people are willing to pay higher prices for them. We make most of our money through selling the babies, but we do a pretty good business with breeding dams from other farms and selling clothing and blankets made from their fleece. Jewel likes that part."

"Did you know this, Monroe?" Melanie asked.

"He keeps me abreast of what's going on."

"My granddad left me fifty acres," Anthony stated. "Since I was the only grandchild who was interested in farming. One day I'd like to buy two or three dams to start my own business. I'm saving up for it. But it takes a while."

"Why don't you get a loan?" Melanie asked. "Or will someone sell you one on a payment plan?"

"I don't want to start off in debt. One thing my granddad taught me was to pay as you go in farming. That's what I plan to do. Of course I've saved almost enough for one already, but they're herd animals. Not good to have one by itself. I was hoping Mr. Bedford lets me keep her here. I'd pay for her food and upkeep."

"That's okay with me," Monroe said. What was one more alpaca? Besides, anything he could do to help the younger man he would. "You want to take off on your own, hmm?" Monroe said. It wouldn't be easy finding another farm manager. Anthony was in charge of everything on the property, including the house, since Monroe was away most of the time. When Monroe had first hired him, he'd been concerned about Anthony's youth, but he'd proved to be worth more than his weight in gold. He was a hard worker.

"Actually I wouldn't need to. Alpacas aren't a lot of work. I could handle my own as well as yours."

Monroe nodded. Maybe he'd sell him one at a discount or give him one as a bonus for sweeping the contest. Eighty grand for one young alpaca was more than enough to earn Anthony a dam. He'd have to get around the Carson pride first. They liked to work for what they made. He only had to look at Melanie to know that.

Although Monroe liked to look at the animals and enjoyed the couple of alpaca sweaters he owned, he didn't love the business the way Anthony did.

Monroe realized that although Anthony came to the farm practically every day, he knew little about the younger man. Didn't know his dreams or even care about why he patiently worked the farm without direction. He always took the lead when he could have done just enough to get by.

Anthony had started out working part-time for Monroe's grandfather. His grandfather had died a year after Anthony had finished college. Monroe knew that Anthony had been away in Peru, but he'd come home for the funeral and had taken over the farm until Monroe had hired him and literally put the farm in Anthony's hands. He deserved more than what he was getting, just for taking the initiative. Anthony didn't have to put out the extra work to raise prize-winning alpacas, but he had— without being told.

Melanie patted her cousin's arm. "Congrats on the win, Anthony."

By the time Eric and Veronica came back from their morning stroll, Ronnie's cheeks were bright, her eyes lively.

"Didn't I see your grandmother?" she asked.

"You missed a lot of people. Melanie came by, too."

"I'm going to finish packing," Ronnie said, running to her room.

When she left, Eric poured himself a cup of coffee. "I want to talk to you alone. But first let me tell you, there wasn't one complaint from Ronnie during our entire stay here. Thanks, man."

Monroe nodded.

"I won't take the position at Emerson unless you do. Are you going to take it? They've thrown in stock options and a seven-figure salary, more than we made when we owned the company."

"I'm not sure."

"What're you going to do, raise alpacas for the rest of your life? Is that what you want?"

"I don't know what I want, okay? And it's for me to figure out."

"You're a scientist. You've got talent most people would kill for. You're going to let this opportunity get away? What a waste."

"I don't need you telling me what to do with my life, okay?"

"Is this going to stand between us forever?"

"No. I realize Peter wanted to leave. And I know I went off on Aaron. So I guess the only alternative was to sell."

"Thanks, man. It means a lot to me. You're my

best friend. Losing your friendship hurt more than selling the business."

Monroe nodded.

"At least go to the meetings. Talk with corporate before you make a decision."

Monroe was quiet. All those old feelings hadn't dissipated, but he couldn't hold on to his anger forever. "Okay." That was the least he could do. It wasn't all about the offer. Despite what he'd told his grandmother, he was thinking about settling down with Melanie.

"I'm ready to go back to work, Monroe. To a job I really enjoy. I think I could make it with this one. The excitement of lazing about on a boat and taking constant trips to the islands wears thin pretty fast. I enjoyed working with you. We worked well together. We understood each other."

Melanie watched a little girl who looked to be around four or five lug an armful of books to the counter and struggle to put them on top. She was so cute, with two pigtails on each side of her head. She had tiny heart earrings in her ears. When her grandmother tried to help her, she refused.

Melanie came around the counter. "What have you here?"

"My grandma's buying all these books just for me."

"You must be a very special little girl to get such wonderful gifts."

The little girl nodded. "I'm going to school next year like my brother. I get to ride the school bus."

"What a big girl you are."

The girl nodded. As Melanie rang up the sale, she remembered how excited Courtney was when she began school. They grow so fast. Every time she blinked, Courtney was going through a new stage. Melanie slipped a set of bookmarks in the girl's bag.

When the little girl left with her grandmother, the last person Melanie expected to see in her store was Mrs. Eudora. Leaving Mrs. Pearl to browse in the Christian book section, Melanie took Mrs. Eudora into the office and fixed her a cup of tea. It seemed like old times having the woman sitting across the desk from her.

Mrs. Eudora seemed agitated. "I just had a fight with Monroe."

"What about?"

"Him and the mayor. Just rattles my teeth the way they're trying to take over my affairs. I've made a decision, Melanie. I've decided to sell the shops at cost to the tenants if they want."

The joy that cascaded over Melanie held no bounds. She brought her hands to her breasts to keep herself planted in her seat and not make an absolute fool of herself. "Do you mean it?"

"Of course."

"Mrs. Eudora. This is the best news. I don't know how to thank you."

"What can I do to help your campaign?" The guarded eyes that met hers were sad.

Melanie's first response was to tell her nothing, to tell her to go home and rest. But she couldn't do that. Mrs. Eudora wanted to be involved.

"I don't know, but I'll need all the help I can get."

She actually smiled. "Well, I'm ready to go anytime you need me."

Melanie hopped around the desk and hugged her.

"Oh, go on with you."

Tears hung on Melanie's eyes. "Thank you," she whispered and kissed the woman's weathered cheek.

"I'm disappointed, you know."

Melanie wondered what she'd done to disappoint the woman. "Why?"

"I was counting on you to keep him here."

She didn't have to ask who "him" was. "I won't stand in his way. I can't. He does important work. How can I keep him from it?"

"Don't you love him?"

The last thing Melanie needed was for Mrs. Eudora to go running back to Monroe telling him Melanie loved him.

"I see it. You feel for him the way I felt for my dear husband."

"Mrs. Eudora…"

"I know what love is. So don't try to pull one over on me," she said with a stubborn tilt to her chin.

"I can't use love to trap him where he doesn't want to be. He's still on the rebound, and he'd hate me for holding him back."

"Oh, pooh. He doesn't love that woman anymore."

"He's found a job he really likes. I see it. He'll always come back. He has a home here." Although she tried to give Mrs. Eudora hope, Melanie knew there was nothing like having family around.

Mrs. Eudora stood. "You're a smart woman, Melanie. He could have done a lot worse than you." She put her purse on her arm. "I was hoping he'd stay."

Melanie hugged the woman and walked her to the office door. When Mrs. Eudora left with Mrs. Pearl, Melanie called all the tenants, announcing an emergency meeting for that night. She had to tell everyone that Monroe hadn't sold.

Melanie wanted to celebrate. She ran to the grocery store and brought fixings for hors d'oeuvres. The table was laden with food when the tenants arrived—from winglets to the deviled eggs Elmore and Uncle Milton loved.

"What's going on?" Uncle Milton said, filling his plate with food.

"Celebrating something?" Elmore asked, placing a couple of deviled eggs on his plate. For the most part, the two men stayed out of each other's way, but the feud was far from over. With the slightest infraction they'd erupt again.

"Yes. And I'll tell you all about it as soon as everyone has filled their plates."

She heard snippets about the investment group she was trying to get to hold the loan. When everyone was seated and began eating, she said, "Mrs. Eudora has offered to sell us the plaza units at cost. She will hold the loan."

"Merciful Jesus," Aunt Thelma cried out. "I knew she was generous, but this—this goes beyond."

"She's given so much. What can we do for her?" Claire asked.

"I've been thinking. What if we named the plaza after her? Bedford's Village Square."

Elmore nodded. "Good idea."

"And we still have to give the anniversary party in her honor," Gail said.

"Of course."

Aunt Thelma nodded. "We're going to make it the grandest event ever, aren't we, Claire?"

"Yes, we are."

Melanie wondered if Monroe would be in town long enough to celebrate with them or if he'd return for the party once he left. She wondered what he thought of his grandmother's generous offer, especially since he'd agreed to do the same thing. But she couldn't accept it from him. After what he'd gone through with Dorian, she couldn't let him believe she wanted him for his money— and that was exactly what he would have believed.

Monroe was so close-mouthed he frustrated her. She knew he felt something for her. But she didn't know if his distrust for women was so deep that it had scarred him for other women.

"Did grandmother talk to you?" Monroe asked the next evening. Melanie was cooking dinner.

"Yes."

"How did the tenants take the news?"

"They're thrilled." Melanie could feel Monroe staring at her. "I know you made the offer, but I couldn't accept it from you."

"Why not?"

"I don't want the man I'm dating to bail me out. When I left Bruce, I promised I'd make it on my own, just like any other single working woman. Can you understand that?"

"It was a business deal. And I'm not Bruce."

"I know you aren't," she said. "You're nothing like him, but mixing business with a personal relationship creates complications. I didn't want business to stand between us."

Using tongs, she took the chicken out of the hot grease and laid it on a plate covered with paper towels. It seemed she and Monroe were growing apart, and he hadn't even left town yet.

Damn it. She was doing it all over again. She was quietly waiting on the sidelines while a man determined her future for her. She was sick of being quiet while the all-important Monroe, Mr. Scientist, made all the decisions. She put several more pieces of chicken in the pan then turned to face Monroe.

"What happens to us when you move?"

"What do you want to happen?" he asked.

She turned, tossed the tongs on the counter. "I hate when you answer a question with a question."

He came behind her, massaged her tense shoulders. "Maybe I'm as tense as you are."

"Why?"

"I'm leaving tomorrow for Philly. Eric and I are meeting with Emerson's management. And I want to know that you'll be here when I return."

Her shoulders sagged. "Where would I go?"

"I don't mean physically. I mean mentally. You seem distant."

"I don't know what you want, Monroe. I'm hanging in limbo here."

"I want you."

"I know you enjoy going to bed with me. But is that all we are?"

"Of course not. I hope I'm more than a bed partner to you."

She sighed. She'd been gearing herself up for the day he told her he was leaving, but actually hearing it was a lot worse than she thought it would be. "How long will you be gone?" she asked quietly.

"A week at the most." He tried to kiss her but she pulled away. He dropped his hands to his sides.

"Whatever I decide to do, we'll find a way to

make our relationship survive. That is, if it's what you want, too." He touched the side of her face lovingly. "I don't want to lose you, Melanie."

She glanced at him. It was the first bit of hope he'd given her that he was ready to put the past completely behind him, that a future was possible. She turned in his arms and laid her head against his chest. "I don't want to lose *you*."

"Come here." His kiss was sweet and tender. It held promises he was unwilling to voice, promises she wasn't ready to trust.

"Do you want me to take you to the airport?" she asked.

"I'll drive. And I'm not sure when I'm coming back."

Monroe had no solution for them, yet. But he knew he couldn't lose Melanie. She was the best thing to ever happen to him.

"What's eating you?" Gail asked two days later.

"Nothing really. Or everything."

"I saw your husband."

"Ex-husband." Melanie scoffed. "Don't forget the *ex*. Big difference."

"Does Monroe know Bruce is here?"

"Monroe left before he arrived. You know,

Monroe calls me every night. The differences between Monroe and Bruce are so sharp. I don't know how I thought I could compare them."

"Why did he come? You always took Courtney to see him."

"The mayor invited him."

"Is he supposed to scare you off from running?"

"I think Bruce forgets that I'm not the same woman who lived with him. He doesn't frighten me."

"One thing's for sure, the mayor's really running scared to send for him. Did you tell Monroe yet?"

"No. I don't want him thinking about Bruce. He isn't part of my life any longer."

"You two had Courtney together—he will always be part of your life."

"If you put it that way." She just wished Bruce would return to D.C. and stay out of her hair. She had enough problems.

Every day apart from Monroe felt like a prelude to when he'd move away forever. She never dreamed she'd love a man the way she loved Monroe, or miss him so intensely. Her heart wanted to take Mrs. Eudora's advice and beg him to stay, but she'd never do that. She'd meant what she'd said to Mrs. Eudora. She'd never hold him back from his goals, from the things that would make him happy and fulfilled.

Even though Monroe had said he wanted to stay in his penthouse condo, Eric and Veronica insisted he spend a few nights at their place. It made it easier for him and Eric to discuss Emerson's offer.

Their son had been happy to see him, and Monroe realized how much he'd missed the boy.

But not nearly as much as he missed Melanie. Each day, his absence from her felt worse; and if it was this sharp now, what would happen when he moved away permanently? He couldn't ask Melanie to leave what was important to her. Especially when it wasn't just her business, but the town's as well.

Monroe and Eric were going over some details before their meeting the next day. Monroe had been tossing ideas around for several days now.

"Eric, is there any reason we can't move the company to Summer Lake?" He finally voiced his desire.

"You want to stay there?"

"The idea's wearing on me. Think about it. Rush hour is nonexistent. Even though it's a small town, the schools are good. Universities and community colleges aren't too far away. We could talk to the city council."

Eric leaned back in his seat. "I'm sure Mrs. Eudora has a lot of pull with them. I can't believe I'm even considering this."

"Grandma's on the city council. Trust me. She has enormous pull."

"And it would boost Melanie's political career, especially with you as campaign manager."

Monroe smiled. "There is that. I don't know. The town's grown on me. It feels like…"

"Like home?"

Monroe nodded.

"I don't know. Good colleges are one thing. But we need experienced experts to feel the same way. How do we convince them to move to the middle of nowhere? Where is the entertainment they're accustomed to? Ronnie mentioned how lovely the town is. But it would be a drastic change."

"We sell it as the perfect small town for families. We tell them they can buy affordable housing without breaking the bank. They'll have more time with their families."

Eric chuckled. "You've already done the marketing?"

"Let's try that angle for one of our options. We

aren't that far from Savannah. Plus as the town grows, so will the variety of entertainment."

"I never even dreamed of moving to a small town."

"Well, if we don't consider Summer Lake, I might not be able to move to another location with the company."

"Melanie means that much to you," Eric said. "All right. You know this is a team effort. Without you, they'll have to spend more than they want to to get this project going."

"At least consider it. That's all I'm asking. We can weigh it against other locations."

Eric shook his head. "I don't know. But I'll talk to Ronnie, see if she'd consider moving there. Convincing me is going to be easier than convincing her. She loves to shop. She loves the theater and concerts."

"She can get all that within an hour's drive, without the traffic jams."

"I owe you this one, don't I?"

"If that's what it takes for you to consider, then yes."

Chapter 12

The last person Melanie expected or wanted to walk into her store was her ex-husband.

"So what brings you here, Bruce?" she asked. He was six feet even and had the handsome face women fell for. Melanie had learned long ago that when the going got rough, handsome didn't cut it. He wore the successful businessman's attire—a Brooks Brothers shirt and linen slacks.

"Are you trying to ignore the fact that I have a daughter here? I'm taking some time off to spend with Courtney."

"I haven't forgotten, but I thought you had. It's about time you spend time with her. Why didn't you call to arrange it with me?"

"What's with the attitude? It doesn't become you." He perused the store in a quick glance. "Cute little place you have here."

"Why, thank you."

"So where's Courtney?"

"In school where most children her age are."

His eyes focused on her again. "How sad. You've become one of those mad single black women."

"If you mean I don't take crap from you any longer, then you're correct."

"I didn't come here to fight, Melanie."

"Good. I'm sure Courtney will be happy to see you. Why don't you find something to do until school's over? Stop by around three-thirty." Melanie wasn't usually sharp, but if she relented even a little, Bruce would yank her chain in every direction. She wasn't going to give him the opportunity, and she was due a few.

He picked up a flyer off the counter. After he read it, he raised an eyebrow. "You're running for mayor?"

"As if you didn't know. You haven't forgotten how to read the paper, have you?" She'd finally gotten to the bottom of the purpose for his visit. Gail had called her earlier when she'd seen Bruce in Andrew's office. The mayor had slipped Bruce into town the same way he'd gone canvassing for buyers for the shopping center. It really ticked her off that Bruce came running into town for the mayor and not for his own daughter.

"What I'm more concerned about is Courtney. How are you going to have enough time to properly care for her if you're running a business along with a mayoral campaign?"

"I know the man who spends no time with his daughter—even when we were married—isn't criticizing my parenting. I spend plenty of time with our daughter. I wasn't the one who refused to spend time with her when I drove her to D.C. on the weekends *you chose*."

He brushed imaginary lint off his shirt. "I had cases to prepare for."

"There was always an excuse. I'd really love to stand in front of a judge and tell her that. You have no time for anyone but yourself and your lady friends."

He tightened his lips. "I don't like your attitude."

"I don't care. It really bugs me that your daughter has always craved your time and you won't give her the time of day. Yet as soon as the mayor calls you, you're down here to stir up trouble, and not to see your daughter, which should be the reason you're here. You're a piece of scum. I can't stand the sight of you. Get out of my store."

The anger poured from him. Melanie thought he was going to work himself into a fit, but he didn't say anything.

"I don't know why, but she wants to see you. I don't."

"You can't talk to me like that." Melanie knew he'd reached his breaking point when his ears turned red.

"I call it the way I see it. Now get out. You aren't fit to be in here. You know, I don't know what I ever saw in you." She turned her back to him and began straightening things on the shelf behind her. When she heard his footsteps cross the floor and the doorbell tingle, she turned back around. Outside her window she saw him stride angrily to his Mercedes and climb in.

Melanie took deep breaths to calm down. Courtney wasn't related to Monroe, yet he coached her soccer team. He'd spent time with her on spring break so she wouldn't be bored in the store, and he'd never complained. Yet Courtney's own father couldn't be bothered with her. He should have asked Courtney to spend spring break with him. Melanie could just smack him.

Monroe called that night, and Melanie was happy to hear his voice.

"I saw Dorian and Aaron today."

"Oh?"

"I thought it best to tie up loose ends. I was bitter before and now... You've helped me with a lot of things."

"How did it go?"

"Okay."

Melanie imagined that if they were going to live in the same city, and since they probably ran in the same circles, they'd run into each other, it was best they cleared the air. But she often wondered if Monroe had any lingering affection for Dorian. Intense dislike sometimes sprang from equally intense love.

"I also talked to the mayor before I left," Monroe said. "As my first official business as campaign manager, I tried to get him to commit to a debate with you."

So that's what frightened Andrew enough to bring Bruce to town. "Isn't it early for a debate?"

"We need to get things rolling if you plan to win this election. He's been mayor for a long time. I imagine a lot of people are so settled they don't bother to even vote. We have to motivate them to go to the polls or he'll win again, by default."

"Has he agreed to a debate?"

"No."

"So much for that."

"Not really. There are ways to maneuver him into a debate. You'll have one before election. Trust me."

"He'll focus on the low crime rate and a family-centered community."

"You'll focus on lack of jobs and ability to raise families."

"While preserving the small-town atmosphere," Melanie agreed. One of the things she liked most about Summer Lake was that it was a caring community. She knew everyone on her road by name. People spoke to her in the grocery store. A hearty conversation could easily get started in the post office.

"Monroe, a small shopping center isn't enough to solve unemployment here. It takes at least one large company that pays decent wages."

"We'll see." A beat of silence spread between them. "Melanie, I know you have a thriving business in Summer Lake. I know you like living there, but do you think you could leave? Do you think you could move to Philly?"

Gosh. Was he asking her to consider marrying him? Or was she jumping to conclusions? Often couples moved in together, but with a daughter, she wouldn't consider that.

"I've never thought about moving," she said, "but I could. I'd have to make a decision quickly since I'm officially running for mayor."

"We'll talk when I get back. Any more incidents with the feud?" He seemed to be jumping from topic to topic.

"There's always a buzz going around town about that. Especially since Thelma and Claire went to the movies together the other night."

"I'd like to be a fly on the wall when Milton and Elmore found out about it."

"I know Aunt Thelma doesn't take any crap from Uncle Milton. He might grumble, but she's going to have her say."

Monroe chuckled.

"Have you seen many of your old friends?"

"Actually, no. I didn't have a lot of friends here other than my partners. I spent most of my time working."

How sad, Melanie thought. A person should have a life outside of work.

"So how are the meetings going?" she asked.

"Tiring, but very productive."

"Maybe I can soothe you when you get back."

His voice lowered almost to a whisper. "Is that a promise?"

She was quiet for two heartbeats before she responded softly. "Definitely a promise." Melanie's heart burned in her chest. Her voice trembled. "Hurry up and get here." Then she hung up before she said too much. She pressed a shaky hand to her breast. Where was he going with all the cryptic messages? Hope blossomed within her, but she could very well be building herself up for the biggest letdown of her life.

Courtney was in seventh heaven because she was going out on a boat with her father. Melanie's happiness was only half-fold. She knew seeing Bruce would only give Courtney false hope that he would stick around. But he was in town and Courtney would feel slighted and hurt if her father paid no attention to her at all.

"Be very careful, Courtney," Melanie said. "Keep your life vest on."

"Oh, Mom. I can swim."

"I know you can. Just humor your mom, okay?"

"You always treat me like a baby."

"I love you, sweetie."

"I know. Can I go now?"

Melanie kissed her, held her tightly in her arms before she released her. "Sure. Have fun."

The weatherman had talked about the storm coming up the east coast for days, but it was charted to go farther out to sea. It was almost upon them when it shifted and passed straight through town. Melanie tried to call Bruce on his cell phone, but she kept getting put into voice mail.

The wind howled, pushing against the car as Melanie drove home. She dialed Bruce's cell phone again, but received no response. Surely he had enough sense to come in off the water when the wind picked up. She dialed the hotel. The desk clerk said he hadn't come back yet.

Melanie drove by the marina. Bruce's car was still parked there, but the wind was rocking so hard, she couldn't stay out in the open. She drove home and called around to see if anyone had seen them. Uncle Milton told her he was going out to look as soon as the storm passed through. Melanie insisted on going with him.

Aunt Thelma told her she and Claire were going to keep calling around.

Once the full force of the storm hit, the wind shook the house and seemed to howl forever. Trees bent, branches snapped. From the window facing the lake, Melanie saw the waves rushing against the shore.

It had been so peaceful earlier in the day. The serene atmosphere was Courtney's favorite thing about living in Summer Lake. Just like Melanie, she loved the water. Loved to swim in it or just to look at it.

Melanie's nerves were frayed to the breaking point as she walked the floor waiting for the storm to end. Her baby was out in this mess. *Please let them have found shelter.*

By the time the search boats were on the water, darkness had almost completely set in. It was still raining, although the wind was nearly quiet. Melanie used one of Uncle Milton's powerful flashlights to scan the water's surface. Several other neighbors had taken their boats out to look for Courtney and Bruce and Melanie could see the lights from a distance. The water was so dark, she struggled to discern anything.

Fear and anxiety burned in her chest as she scanned the water and saw nothing except the waves churning underneath. Every time she saw something bobbing in the water, a glimmer of hope soared, until it turned out to be a piece of driftwood or other debris.

It was completely dark now, and there was no dark like the dark of a country night with clouds hovering overhead. Not a single star lit the sky.

Due to the storm, Monroe's plane was late arriving in Savannah. He was tired as heck after the long days he and Eric had put in, but it had been worth every minute. He had gotten what he wanted: the company was setting up shop in Summer Lake.

Even Veronica was amenable to living in a smaller community, although she worried about missing the cultural activities she enjoyed in Philly.

On his way home, Monroe drove over broken branches and swerved around fallen trees. He dialed Melanie's number.

She picked up the phone immediately. "Hello?" her anxious voice came over the wire.

"What's wrong, honey?"

"Courtney went boating with Bruce and they're missing."

"Are they getting a search party together?"

"We've been out." Her anguished voice crushed his heart. "He knows the lake fairly well. Except it's dark and hard to see. I'm going out again as soon as we discuss how to continue the search."

"I'm almost there."

The search team had come in, but the patrol boat was still out there. They found a capsized boat, but no passengers.

Melanie was frantic with worry. Her only hope was that Courtney had actually worn a life jacket. Surely Bruce wouldn't let the child ride in a small boat without one.

When Monroe arrived, she fell into his arms but held back tears. She had to keep her mind clear so she could think straight.

"I'm going to get my boat and go out," Monroe said. He gave her a quick hug. Before he left, he said a few words to Mrs. Eudora, who was worriedly handing out coffee.

Uncle Milton got a cup of coffee and walked over to his niece.

Elmore squeezed Melanie's hand and left with his boys.

"That's a crying shame. Here you're sick with worry and Elmore's just gone and deserted you. After all you've done for him," Uncle Milton said.

"I don't want to hear about the feud. I want my baby!" Melanie said, finally bursting into tears. Aunt Thelma threw a look at her husband and gathered Melanie into her arms.

"There, there. The men are going back out. They're gonna check every inch of that lake."

Melanie swiped a hand across her eyes. "I need to go out. I can't just sit in here."

"You stay right here. The men are going to take care of everything."

"I have to go, Aunt Thelma. It'll drive me crazy standing around, waiting."

Uncle Milton came over. "Come on." Melanie grabbed her waterproof jacket and followed him.

Summer Lake was dark and bleak, and although on land the air was warm, on the lake it was cold. Melanie pulled her windbreaker tightly around her. Courtney was wet and cold, shivering somewhere on the water. *Please let her have worn her life jacket.*

Her flashlight beaming on the water, Melanie

looked out onto the inky surface, hoping to see an orange life jacket bobbing in the waves. She saw nothing but the relentless surface. They stayed out for hours. Melanie knew Uncle Milton and his sons had given up finding anything. They were there only to appease her. A few hours later, they docked the boat. Melanie's heart was heavy with pain. Anyone who said a heart didn't hurt didn't know what he was talking about. She felt as if somebody had stuck a knife in her heart and slowly twisted it. They had no more than walked the deck to shore when Melanie's cell phone rang. Grasping it from her pocket, she flipped it open. It was Monroe.

"We found them. Courtney and Bruce are fine. But Elmore got hurt rescuing them. We're on our way to the hospital."

"How bad is he?"

"Pretty bad, Melanie."

"I'm on my way."

"They found them. But Elmore's badly injured. They're on their way to the hospital," she told the others.

Uncle Milton and his boys drove her to the hospital. There they found Courtney and Bruce wrapped in warm blankets. Courtney ran to Melanie and she closed her arms around her child, a huge weight lifting from her chest. Courtney's hair was a mess, and she shivered in Melanie's arms, but her baby was alive.

"Mama, we hit something and the boat turned over. I flew through the air. It scared me to death."

Melanie trembled and held her child close.

Courtney pushed back. "We were in the water forever. And it was cold."

"Are you okay now?" Melanie looked her over to assure herself that she was.

"I'm warm now. I didn't get hurt."

Melanie squeezed her once more. She was still shaking from the ordeal. "Honey, sit here. Let me find out about Mr. Hicks." Melanie approached Monroe and Elmore's sons. Claire hadn't arrived yet.

"He's in surgery," Monroe said. "There is internal bleeding, as well as some broken bones." Monroe looked as haggard as the boys. They had warm blankets wrapped around them, too. Melanie hugged the boys and said a prayer.

"I'm so sorry about Elmore," she said. "Words won't express how very, very grateful I am. Thank you."

"Dad thinks a lot of you, Melanie. He woulda done anything for you."

Melanie prayed that didn't include giving his life. Courtney came over beside her and they got the boys coffee while they waited. When Connie arrived with her mother, Courtney went to sit with her. She noticed that Bruce had already slunk away.

"Everything okay at the farm?" Uncle Milton asked the Hicks boys.

"We've got to go and see about the animals. Didn't have time to earlier."

"Don't you worry about that," Uncle Milton said. "Stay with your mama. She'll be here soon. Me and my boys'll take care of the farm." Uncle Milton turned to leave.

"You'll need the keys," the young man said.

Uncle Milton turned as Elmore's son dug into his pocket and dropped a set of keys in his hand.

Shock froze everyone in place. Conversations stopped. Noise diminished to nothingness. Melanie nearly dropped her coffee. Uncle Milton offering to do something for a Hicks. And lightning didn't strike him dead.

He must have felt the curiosity in the room because his eyes avoided Melanie's and everyone else's as he and his sons left. Only then did shocked conversations resume.

Never thought I'd see the day. As I live and breathe, were only some of the phrases Melanie caught.

Gail approached her. "I'm going to take Courtney home with me. She can stay with me, or with my sister if she wants to be around other kids. She looks really tired. And I know you're going to be here a while."

Courtney was sitting in a corner with Connie. Melanie really didn't want her child out of her sight, but she didn't know how long they'd be at the hospital. When Gail approached Courtney, the child ran to Melanie.

"I want to stay with Connie, Mom. Can I, please?" Courtney said. "She's really upset about her grandfather. And I'm worried, too."

"Of course, sweetheart." Courtney dashed back over to console Connie. "She'll be all right here," Melanie told Gail.

"Then I'll stay a while in case she changes her mind."

Melanie sat beside Gail and it wasn't long before Monroe sat on the other side and took her hand, giving her comfort as they waited.

Mrs. Claire arrived and Aunt Thelma sat with her.

Elmore was in surgery six hours. By the time

the doctor came out, Uncle Milton and his boys had returned.

Everyone tensed until the doctor told them the surgery had gone well. There was a collective sigh of relief. But Elmore wasn't out of the woods quite yet. He'd be in intensive care for a couple of days at least.

Melanie felt as if someone had picked her up and squeezed her dry.

Uncle Milton offering to see to the farm while Elmore was in the hospital gave Melanie a glimmer of hope that the feud would end. But why did a tragedy have to occur before the man changed? At least she hoped he'd changed—that he wouldn't go back to his old ways once Elmore was back on his feet. Only time would tell.

Anthony came up to the house and knocked on Monroe's door.

"I'm going to leave for a little while and help with the morning feeding at the Hicks farm. I've already fed the alpacas and I've checked them over to make sure they're okay."

"Fine, but you don't need to check in with me."

"Well, since you were here…"

"Just do things as you do when I'm away. I'm

glad you're here, though. I wanted to talk with you a moment."

"Okay." Anthony came into the house and closed the door behind him.

"I was thinking that you've done a great job with the alpacas, especially considering that you've had no supervision."

Anthony nodded. "You've got a great herd. One to be proud of."

"How many alpacas did we have when you took over?"

"Around fifteen."

"And it's grown to fifty already?"

"I wrote you letters telling you that I was using the profits to buy additional alpacas. And I didn't sell all of the offspring each year. I was trying to build up the herd. I hope it's not a problem."

"On the contrary. You've succeeded too well. I've been thinking you deserve a bonus. How about I give you half of the profit from the breeding of our prize-winning alpacas, and sell you as much of the herd as you want—at half price?"

Anthony looked as if he were going to faint. "But…but that's too generous."

"If you weren't so conscientious, we wouldn't

have made nearly as much. The herd wouldn't be nearly as large." Monroe extended a hand for a shake.

Anthony pumped his hand eagerly and smiled. "I never dreamed…"

"As soon as we sell the young ones, you'll get that bonus."

"I can't believe it." He shook his head and repeated, "I just can't believe it."

Monroe's gesture wasn't totally altruistic. He figured with the bonuses, Anthony would be more likely to continue to work the alpacas when he began his own farm. Monroe didn't even want to begin to think about having to find a replacement. It was a stroke of luck for him to have Anthony in the first place.

"And I want to be the first one to buy two of your crias."

"A sale is a sale."

"I never dreamed I'd be able to buy them so quickly." He headed to the door. "I won't be gone long."

"Take all the time you need."

As Monroe watched Anthony leave, he wished it would be as easy dealing with Melanie. It felt good doing something positive for another person.

* * *

Monroe's grandmother had called and he stood by her house. He found her sitting on the porch with a tall glass of lemonade. Mrs. Pearl brought out a glass for him. The day was hot and the drink hit the spot.

"How did the trip go?" she asked.

"Fine."

"So you're going to take the job?"

"We'll see." He could see the disappointment on her face. "I'm not deserting you," he said, but he didn't want to reveal anything until after he spoke with Melanie.

If his grandmother's chin got any higher, it was going to touch the ceiling. "Don't let me stand in your way. I can take care of myself."

"I know." He'd gotten used to her. He didn't want to leave her alone. She should be surrounded by family.

"Your sister called."

"What did she want?"

"She's coming for the Fourth. Said she was staying a month."

"You're kidding."

"Nope. Shocked me, too. Remember when she said she wasn't going to ever let any grass grow under her feet?"

"She meant every word."

"You got that right. I meant to tell you, I think I lost a few years when Courtney went missing. I hope Bruce leaves and never comes back."

"You know how the wind can pick up over the lake. It's happened to me. Besides, the boat capsized when it hit a log. Can't blame him for that."

"I can blame him for anything I want. He should have been paying attention. But I blame the mayor most of all. Getting Courtney all worked up and Bruce probably won't visit her again for another year or two. The only time he sees her is when Melanie takes her to see him."

Monroe shook his head and glanced fondly at his grandmother. "He's missing a lot. Courtney's a wonderful little girl."

Soon after the boating accident, the mayor made a hasty retreat out of town with the excuse that his wife needed a vacation. Many people, especially Uncle Milton, blamed the accident on him, even though it was obviously not his fault. Melanie tried to dissuade them from blaming anyone, but they continued to say that if he hadn't called Bruce, he and Courtney wouldn't have been out on the lake. Melanie countered with the fact that she had asked Bruce to spend time with Courtney, so it was more her fault. But when did Uncle Milton ever listen to her? Now that the feud was unofficially over, he had to have someone to fight with.

The whole situation was giving Melanie a headache.

Monroe came by her house after Courtney's bedtime.

"Things are finally settling down, thank goodness. The whole town is buzzing with your generosity to Anthony. He is so thrilled."

"Nothing more than he deserves." Monroe leaned against the counter.

Melanie approached him and laid her hand against his chest. "You've got quite a heart in there."

"You think so?" He pressed his hand over hers and she felt the rapid beat.

"I think you have a lot of your grandmother's generous spirit."

"With you standing so close and smelling so good, I'm beginning to think of only you."

Melanie linked her hands around his neck and lowered his head for her kiss. How she loved that man.

"With all that's going on we haven't had time

to discuss your trip," Melanie said when they were both heated. "How was it?"

"Better than expected."

"You accepted?"

"It's provisional. I told them I would only accept it if they built the subsidiary here."

Melanie's heart leaped in her chest. "Here? In Summer Lake?"

Monroe nodded. "They're doing a study to see if it's possible. They also have a terrific benefits and stock-options package," he said. "Maybe I needed to go through the trauma of the last two years so that I could appreciate what you mean to me," he said.

Melanie sat before she fell.

"If I'd met you years ago, we wouldn't have lasted. There wouldn't have been other women, but I was so absorbed in my work, there wouldn't have been room for a family. I would have neglected you the way I neglected Dorian. I needed this chance to grow."

"Hey, we don't get test runs in life. We learn as we go. Believe me, I've made my share of mistakes."

"I left a door wide open for Aaron to walk into my home like a thief." He curled a lock of her sable hair around his finger. "I'm a different man. You've destroyed my shadows."

"What?"

He took Melanie's hand in his. "I promise you, I'll be an attentive husband. If you marry me."

Startled, Melanie's gaze jerked to his.

"Will you marry me, Melanie?"

"I thought…"

"What?"

She smiled. Her hands trembled as she held them together.

"Do you love me?" she asked.

"Is there any doubt? I've juggled my world to fit yours."

She closed her eyes briefly. She'd never thought to hear him say he loved her. "I love you, Monroe. Yes. I'll marry you."

"Melanie, I have to go before the city council. We have a lot of work ahead of us and we still might not be able to build Emerson's subsidiary here."

"You can't work out all the problems ahead of time."

"I need to work. In my field."

"If you have to leave, I'll leave with you," Melanie promised.

"But the town needs you."

"*I* need *you*. And who says it won't work out? We need a company like Emerson here. Small towns have to find a way to create jobs to keep their own. It's no longer a farming community. We have to find other ways to support it. The town can't rely on other places to support them. People are going to find a way to provide for their families. Either we bring legitimate jobs, or they will go somewhere else."

"I'll pick you up early tomorrow so we can tell Eudora together. We'll bring Courtney."

"You want to shock her at breakfast?"

"The old grouch needs a shock."

Melanie chuckled.

"Can't you see it? We'll need a nice hotel, more restaurants. More jobs. I think it's time for the residents of Summer Lake to move into the twenty-first century—and that is what I'm going to build my campaign on."

"Congratulations, Madam Mayor." Monroe loved to hear her talk and dream. He pulled her into his arms and kissed her. "I've never kissed a budding politician before."

Melanie linked her arms around his neck. "Maybe you need practice."

"Umm. Lots of practice." The distance

between their mouths diminished until his lips were just a whisper away. "No reason we can't start now."

Big-boned beauty, Chere Adams
plunges headfirst into an
extreme makeover to impress
fitness fanatic
Quentin Abrahams.

But perhaps it's Chere's curves that
have caught Quentin's eye?

All About Me

Marcia
King-Gamble

AVAILABLE JANUARY 2007
FROM KIMANI™ ROMANCE

Love's Ultimate Destination

Available at your favorite retail outlet.